PIRATE TREASURE OF CAPE MAY

This story is dedicated to all those who forgo a sit-com or video game and pick up a book instead.

Illustrations by Frank DiGregorio

© by Steve Leadley 2008

ISBN#: 9781980782230

A Beach Reeds Publication

1

The Way To Cape May

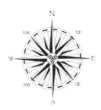

The tires gave off a monotonous hum as the minivan cruised south along the Garden State Parkway. Traffic was light since relatively few people made the trek to the Jersey shore this early in the spring.

"They're the smart ones," Max thought as he rested his head on the passenger side window. He leaned back to watch the telephone lines dance along above him against the backdrop of an overcast sky.

"Are we almost there?" drifted from the back seat, almost pleading in anticipation.

"No," Max grunted rudely to his seven-year-old sister. "And stop asking."

"Have you been checking the side of the road?" their mother asked from the driver's seat, ignoring her son's brusque attitude.

"I can't see from here. I'm too short with the seatbelt on." Brooke strained at the strap, as she tried to examine the shoulder.

"Max, do you see any white sand along the side?" their mother queried.

"No." came the curt reply.

"Mom, he didn't even look!"

"I don't have to. You always said that when we get close to the shore there's white sand on the shoulder because people's tires pick up sand in beach towns and it gets kicked out as they go fast on the highway, right? Well we're on south side of the parkway heading *toward* the shore. Any white sand would be on the other side, from the people going home," the unpleasant boy defended himself.

The tale had been one their mother had employed for years to quell that phrase that all parents dread: "Are we there yet?"

"Well I don't know about that, Mr. Smartypants. Don't you think some people come to the Jersey shore *from* the south? They might take the ferry across the Delaware Bay and vacation in Ocean City or Sea Isle and then head back south toward the ferry again to get home," their ever upbeat mother shot back with a smile.

"Yeah, that's right!" Brooke added, optimistically.

Max merely sniffed his disbelief.

"I just saw a sea gull!" Brooke exclaimed.

"See, we *are* getting close." Their mother smiled, tooting the horn in celebration. The little girl in the back seat giggled.

Max was still simmering over the fact that his mother did not allow them to bring their mp3 players, hand-held video games, or any other electronic form of entertainment.

"You know," Max interjected. "This trip would've gone by a lot faster if we could've brought the portable dvd player."

"I told you Max," his mother replied with a smile. "This is an *adventure weekend*. We're going to explore Cape May! There's the lighthouse, the World War Two bunker, the concrete ship...hey I even heard that there's a secret tunnel under Congress Hall. Maybe I can talk somebody into letting us check it out!"

Their mom had always been great at coming up with unique and creative "adventures." In the past, she would declare it was time for a "mystery ride" and they would pile into the car and end up at some unusual location. Sometimes it would be the shore, other times a museum. Occasionally the destination would be a historic site like Batsto Village or Washington's Crossing. Other times she would wake up early and hide some item in the house or yard and draw up a treasure map. On still other occasions she would make up a list of different kinds of leaves, rocks, and birds and they would go on a scavenger hunt in the woods.

Max and Brooke's dad had passed away just after Brooke was born, so the three of them were often alone, and their mom's excursions had always proved both fun and educational. However, Max had recently become increasingly less enthused

3

with these types of activities. The fact was that he was growing up, and began to resent time away from his friends, particularly if that time had to be spent with his mother and sister. He still loved them, but he was eleven years old now, and becoming more and more interested in "boy things." His mom was creative and entertaining, but she had no experience with, or interest in, sports or video games. Where Max had once considered his mom to be exciting, he began to think of her eccentricities as scatterbrained and flighty.

"Brooke can you see that sign?" her mom asked, pointing ahead.

The little girl anxiously leaned over and peered through the windshield. "Parkway ends 1,000 feet!" she read with enthusiasm. "We're almost there!"

A moment later the dinosaur bridge that separates the beginning of the Cape May Canal from the harbor was behind them and the car was decelerating to twenty-five miles per hour as they entered the quaint Victorian town. As the minivan crept down Lafayette Street, mom and daughter began pointing out different historic homes, debating which of the pastel and gingerbread trimmed buildings they liked best.

The family had visited Cape May before, but this was their first trip staying in town alone. A friend of their mother had inherited a very small cottage years before and they had often vacationed with the divorcee and her two children. Their mother's friend, Mandy, had given them use of the little bungalow on this overcast and gloomy March weekend.

The minivan swung in off of the street and the clamshells that made up the short driveway of the cottage crackled and popped under the tires. With a screech, the vehicle jolted to a halt.

"We're here!" their mother announced, tooting the horn.

Brooke scrambled to unfasten her seatbelt but Max had not removed his head from the side window. Through its reflection he could see the buds that were just forming on the wispy tops of the old maple trees that lined the street. Suddenly he heard a loud rush as the branches thrashed violently from a powerful gust of wind. The breeze was so strong that it held the door fast as Brooke wrestled to get out of the car.

"Max, help with the suitcases," his mom called from the front porch.

As Max stepped from the auto he looked around suspiciously, wondering where the odd blast of air had come from; however all was quiet. He lugged two large suitcases (far too large for a weekend stay, he thought) up the single step and across the small porch. He deposited them heavily on the living room floor and sunk into a wicker chair.

"There's still another one!" his mother called from the kitchen where she was stocking the refrigerator from the cooler she had carried inside.

With an aggravated sigh, Max hauled himself out of his seat and trudged back to the car. As he did, he was nearly lifted off of his feet by another gust of wind that seemed to come upon him like a phantom. But like the last, this squall disappeared as quickly as it had arrived. Max gazed up at the gray mass that covered the sky. The entire field was a light gray without even a hint of blue. Darker, charcoal colored vapors raced quickly across the sky below the dull tin ceiling above. As he walked back with the suitcase, his mother stepped out onto the porch to lock the car with her remote. As he passed the windshield, a fat drop of rain plopped on the glass.

"Gee you picked a heck of a weekend to visit!" A voice drifted over the picket fence that separated the little bungalow from the large Victorian home next door.

"Oh, hello Mr. Jacobs!' Max's mom called back to the elderly man approaching the fence.

Max and Brooke's mother had known the old widower since she was a little girl. She and Mandy had been friends since childhood and had vacationed with Mandy's grandparents several times each summer. Occasionally the kind neighbor had even babysat them when Mandy's grandparents had gone out for the evening.

Mr. Jacobs had grown up in Cape May and had lived alone in the big elegant house for many years. Even though Max's mom had known him for most of her life, he was already a widower by the time she first met him. He was an impressive gardener and although his yard teemed with flowers during the summer months, it was surprising how many plants he was able to coax into blooming this early in the season. His kind face and snowy white hair and beard made it impossible to tell just how old he was, but he must have been quite old since their mother said she couldn't ever remember him looking differently. Although he spent most of his time quietly gardening, Mandy's grandparents had always called him "the best neighbor in the world." Since he lived in Cape May all year, he compassionately kept an eye on the little cottage during the off-season. Mandy's grandparents had even given him a key. Even after Mandy had inherited the little cottage he continued to look after the place. Just last winter a water pipe had burst and Mr. Jacobs was on the spot to not only shut off the water, but he also arranged for a plumber to do the repair work, saving Mandy the long trip to the shore.

"Didn't you listen to the weather?" he asked with a chuckle, as he rested the potted plant he had been carrying on the fence post.

"Well actually, not since earlier in the week." Max's mom confessed, walking over to their side of the fence.

Max rolled his eyes. Just like his mother, he thought.

"We're in for a nor'easter. I think you'd better batten down the hatches!" The gentleman laughed as he removed his round wire-rimmed glasses and cleaned them with his shirttail.

"Well that will add some adventure to our weekend, won't it?" she poked a finger in Max's shoulder.

"Seriously though," Mr. Jacobs's face lost its merriment. "If that little house starts to shake, you're welcome to come over.

7

My house was built in 1870 by a retired sea captain and it's seen its share of nor'easters and hurricanes alike."

"Okay, thanks Mr. Jacobs," Max's mother replied, even though she wasn't the least bit concerned.

Max followed his mother back into the little abode. He was in the bedroom, in the process of carelessly tossing his clothes from his suitcase into the dresser drawers when he heard his mother in panic in the kitchen. He poked his head out of the doorway to see her digging through her purse. She emptied the contents onto the table and shuffled frantically through the pile. Next she did the same to her overnight bag. She obviously hadn't found what she was looking for as she scurried into her own bedroom and dismantled the contents of her suitcase. Finally she addressed the children.

"Have either of you seen my check?" she asked in exasperation.

"Nope!" Brooke replied, without looking up from her coloring book.

"Your paycheck?" Max asked.

"Yes, I thought I put it in my purse before we left."

"No, I saw it on the refrigerator as we were leaving," Max returned.

"Oh, darn it! I forgot it! I was going to cash it over at the bank when we got down here. I only have five dollars!"

"Well you've got your credit cards right?" Max intelligently deduced.

"Yes, but I can't put anything else on them right now," she sighed. She slumped into a chair, her chin on her chest. Being a single parent could be difficult, in more ways than one. Their mother never wanted her children to have less than their friends so she tried her best to buy them the toys and gadgets the other kids had. Unfortunately, this left her credit cards nearly maxed out. She had specifically set aside a portion of her paycheck for the "adventure weekend" and now she had gone and forgotten it at home. Their mother was the type who couldn't be kept down for long, though. Where others might see the glass half empty, she considered it half full. Even though she looked defeated at the moment, Max knew that she was calculating a plan of action. His suspicions were confirmed when she sprang up a moment later and bounded out the door.

"Watch Brooke for me Max, I'll be right back," she called over her shoulder.

Five minutes later their mother was back through the door, and the blast of wind that followed her rifled the pages of Brooke's coloring book. Their mother actually had to struggle with the door to get it to close.

"Okay, I have to go home and get that check. I should be back in a little over three hours. Mr. Jacobs has agreed to watch you while I go," she announced. Her attitude was buoyant as ever, despite the unpleasant task ahead of her.

"Oh Mom, you're kidding right?" Max groaned. "I can watch us!"

"No, that won't do. He is a very nice man. I've known him practically my whole life. He's doing us a tremendous favor. You complained about the hour and a half drive down here, do you really want to come all the way back with me?" She uncharacteristically ranted, with more than a hint of annoyance in her voice. In the blink of an eye however, she was back to her positive self. "I said we were going to have an adventure weekend, and I'll be darned if we don't!" She mussed Brooke's hair and gave her a wink. Her daughter beamed in reply, thankful that their weekend would not have to be aborted. "I'll tell you what-- if the storm blows over, you can go up to the arcade. I'll leave my last five dollars with you."

Their mother led the ever-optimistic Brooke and the truculent Max over to the big Victorian home next door, and after trading her cell phone number for Mr. Jacobs' house exchange, she raced between the raindrops and vaulted into the minivan. Max watched through the big picture window as her taillights vanished down the street.

"Would you two like some cookies? I believe I have some around here somewhere!" Mr. Jacobs called over his shoulder as he retreated to the kitchen.

"Yeah!" Brooke exclaimed her approval of the idea.

Max turned from the window and flopped onto an ornate sofa. He sat with his arms crossed, surveying his surroundings. The large living room was decorated with expensive furniture and draperies. Crystal knickknacks lined one high shelf. The room

10

itself was quite large and the ceiling was easily ten feet high. At the far side of the room, on the wall that comprised the east end of the building sat a large fireplace with a delicately and elaborately carved mantel of expensive mahogany. Above the hearth was a beautiful and intricate mirror. In an adjacent corner, the pendulum from a grandfather clock clicked noisily too and fro. Not only was the décor expensive, but it all appeared to be vintage antiques.

"Here you are." Mr. Jacobs roused Max from his inspection as he placed a tray on the carved table beside them. "Sugar cookies and some milk for my guests," he smiled at them.

"Thanks," Max muttered through a sour complexion.

"Umm. These are gooood!" Brooke approved after taking a bite.

"Do you have a TV?" Max asked, without revealing that he too found the cookies delicious.

"Sure, come on in the library. Right this way." Mr. Jacobs lifted the tray and walked across the large hall that bisected the house, and past the wide staircase. "Can you give me a hand here please Max?" he asked, using his free hand to slide open one of the large oak pocket doors leading into the room. Max complied, heaving the companion door open. Inside was another well furnished room with a sofa, a settee, and an overstuffed chair, all arranged on a large oriental carpet. The far wall had another large fireplace that mirrored the design of the one in the living room. The other walls were covered with built-in bookcases from floor to ceiling.

"There must be a hundred books!" Max thought to himself.

He noticed other items on the shelves besides books, though. There were several framed pictures. One was of a young man in a military uniform. The picture looked old, but it was in color, so it couldn't have been that old, he deduced. There was also another photograph, this one in black and white, of a young man and woman sitting in the house's garden. Max walked over for a closer look and he could see that the man was obviously Mr. Jacobs, although his hair was dark and he was clean-shaven. Another picture stood nearby of a boy about Max's age sitting on the beach with his arm around a girl near Brooke's age. A thin bouquet of dried flowers had been placed across the bottom of the frame. On the other side of the room another shelf was conspicuously vacant of books. On it rested a bell a little bigger than a grapefruit in size, and a large brownish bottle. On the wall beside this case was a framed diploma from the University of Pennsylvania.

"Here's the television young man." Mr. Jacobs interrupted the boy's inspection as he opened a cabinet built into the lower level of the bookcase.

Sheets of rain began to noisily spray the windows. The old host glanced outside with a disapproving expression before continuing over to Max. "Here's the remote," he said, handing the device to the boy.

"Thanks," Max replied, legitimately grateful. The one bright spot in the whole trip was that now he had a TV to watch. No sooner had he clicked it on however, than a tremendous explosion was heard outside, followed by a devastating flash of lightning. The thunderclap had been so loud Max jumped a foot off of the ground, and Brooke began to cry. On the heels of the blast, all of the lights cut out.

Mr. Jacobs scurried to the window. "It hit the transformer on the pole across the street. Its okay, don't be afraid, Brooke." he said, patting her head as she clung to her brother. "I'll get some candles and light a fire in the fireplace." Mr. Jacobs disappeared from the room as an aggravated Max tossed the useless remote onto the sofa, gritting his teeth.

Although the storm had darkened the sky, it was still only ten o'clock in the morning, so the room was dim, but it wasn't pitch-black. Once Mr. Jacobs had lit a fire in the hearth, candles really weren't necessary. The thunder continued, accompanied by howling winds, as the children sat morosely on the sofa. As the kindly old man finished kindling the fire he turned to catch the dismal expressions on their faces.

"What to do? What to do on such a day?" he chuckled, attempting to dispel their anxiety. The old man tapped his forefinger on his pursed lips. "What if I told you a story?" he raised his eyebrows.

"Oh great," Max muttered under his breath.

"If I tell you though, you have to swear not to repeat it. You see it's a secret. In fact, it's a true story." The old man's expression grew solemn.

Despite pretending otherwise, Max was a bit intrigued. Brooke had likewise stopped crying and her positive countenance had revived.

"What's it about?" Brooke smiled, wiping her eyes.

"Well," Mr. Jacobs leaned close, "pirates," he nearly whispered.

"Pirates!" Brooke bounced in her seat.

"Well, mostly pirate treasure," he winked back. "Do you like pirate stories?"

"Oh yes. Max, tell him how many times you saw the *Pirates of the Caribbean* movies!" Brooke affirmed.

"Did you know that in the late sixteen hundreds and early seventeen hundreds Cape May was a frequent stop for pirates?" Mr. Jacobs asked.

"Really?" Brooke asked, wide-eyed.

Max had begun to creep forward on the couch. "Yes, they used to ambush ships headed up the Delaware Bay to Philadelphia, right?"

"That's right. Have you ever heard of Captain Kidd?" A flash of lightning and crash of thunder eerily punctuated the old man's question.

At mention of the infamous pirate's name both children leaned forward, their eager faces tinted by the flames that danced in the fireplace.

"There is a local legend about a certain tree…well hold on a minute…" he trailed off as he walked past the fire to one of the high bookcases. "Hmm," he said, scanning the shelves. "Ah, here it is." He pulled a volume and thumbed through the index and marked a page with his thumb. "Here we are, read this," he directed, handing the open book to Max.

"For many years a gnarled tree stood in Cape May Point that was known as Captain Kidd's Treasure Tree. It was rumored that the tree indicated where the famous pirate had buried his treasure," Max read aloud.

"Captain Kidd's tree? Wow, is there treasure there?" Brooke enthusiastically asked over the sound of the rain pelting the windows.

"No treasure was ever found there, but remember what Max read. He said that the tree *indicated where the treasure was.* For many years people took that to mean that the treasure was buried at the tree. However, what if by *indicate* the legend means *shows?*"

"So, by examining the tree, somebody might learn where the treasure really is!" Max let his excitement escape.

"Unfortunately, that's not possible. The tree was cut down many, many years ago."

"Oh." The dejected kids sighed in unison.

15

Mr. Jacobs walked over to the window, and surveyed the tempest outside. His smile was imperceptible to the pair. "There was a boy about your age Max, and come to think of it he had a sister right around your age, Brooke. Rumor has it that they found a clue that led to another and then to another…"

"Did they find the treasure?" Brooke exploded.

"Would you like me to tell you what happened?" he asked, turning from the window.

"*Please!*" Brooke begged.

"How about you, Max?" the old man queried.

"Sure." Max tried ineffectively to mask his eagerness.

"Alright, but first I have to ask," the old man's features became somber as the flames reflected off of his glasses. "You're not afraid of ghosts are you?"

2

The Hidden Passage

It was a few years after World War II had ended, and Cape May was finally getting back to normal. The lookout towers that had scanned the Atlantic for Hitler's U-boats were no longer manned, and the bunker guarding the entrance to the Delaware Bay had been deactivated. Soldiers were now returning back to the United States in droves, enthusiastically reuniting with their best girl. The couples were eager to begin families, a dream that had sustained both soldier and sweetheart during the long fretful separation. The Jersey shore would again be a popular destination for vacationers, and as summer approached, the hotels and businesses of Cape May readied for the anticipated invasion.

"Billy!" the woman called out through the screen door, wiping her hands on her apron.

"Yeah Ma?" the boy yelled back from the driveway, poking his head over the upside down bicycle he had been oiling.

"Billy, come here a minute, please." The pleasant voice drifted over the picket fence separating the back yard from the garage.

"What is it Ma?" the boy asked, leaning on the gate.

"I met a young couple in the grocery store this morning. They just bought the old Bennett place. They need help cleaning out the basement. I told them you would go over after lunch."

"Aw Ma," the boy whined, adjusting his red baseball cap with oily fingers. "Do I have to?"

"Yes. It's the neighborly thing to do." she replied, without altering her soft, agreeable tone. "They said they would pay you, too." She smiled, knowing that this addendum would alter her son's opinion.

"Really? How much?" he inquired sprightly as he stepped through the gate and approached the screen door.

"Oh, I believe the gentleman said three dollars."

"Three dollars! Oh boy! I'll be able to get that slingshot!"

It was no secret that Billy had been salivating over a slingshot in the Sears catalog. Several of the local boys had them and had been entertaining themselves by trying to bull's-eye rats over at Schellenger's Landing, where the commercial fishing boats were moored.

Typical of mothers, she was uneasy about such activities. However, her husband had reassured her that boyhood was fraught with such adventures and misadventures, and that if their son only wanted to plink a few rats down at the wharf, they should consider themselves lucky. He reminded her that when he was a boy he had found some unexploded World War I grenades and used them to "fish" in Cape May harbor.

"Is lunch ready? I want to get over there and get to it," Billy asked as he entered the house.

"Lunch is on the table, but don't you sit down until you go wash up. You're covered in grease. Tell Mary that lunch is ready on your way to the bathroom."

Billy and his younger sister ate at very different paces. The little girl hummed a tune as she casually dipped her bread in the bowl of tomato soup. Her brother however, devoured the sandwich with the audacity of a buzz saw and then picked up the container of soup in both hands and drank it down. Ordinarily, his mother would not have tolerated such ill manners, but knowing that her volunteering the boy was the cause of his haste, she let it go with a quiet smile.

"When is Daddy coming home?" the little girl asked, absently dunking her crust.

"Not for another few days," their mother replied. As a commercial fisherman, their father was often away for several weeks at a time.

"All done," Billy matter-of-factly stated, looking to his mother for confirmation.

"Alright. Go and wash your face, it's covered in soup, and then head on over. By the way," she called after him as he exploded out of his seat. "The couple's name is Mr. and Mrs. Oakley!"

19

Billy ran a washcloth over his face and sped out to the garage. He flipped his bicycle upright and began running down the driveway, leaping aboard like a stunt rider at the rodeo. He cranked his way down Washington Street, waving to Mr. Mickle the postman as he sped past the Physick mansion. He snaked his way around a few potholes and jumped the curb at Hughes Street, before screeching to a halt in front of the old Bennett house. Like so many homes in Cape May, it had been built during the Victorian era. Yet it was not typical. It was a large house to be sure, but hardly opulent. It was not festooned with decorative brick-a-brack like its neighbors. The white paint was somewhat dingy, and was peeling in many places. The faded trim was not a vibrant pastel, but rather a simple green. Although the house had been in the Bennett family for generations, it had been vacant for almost four years. Thomas Bennett, the previous owner, had been killed at Iwo Jima and his widow had moved to Philadelphia to be with her own family.

Billy leaned his bike against the wrought iron fence and hopped up the steps to the double front doors. He knocked rather forcefully on the solid wood until he heard footsteps on the other side.

"Why hello," The attractive face of a young woman poked her head through the opening. "You must be Billy." She offered her hand as she stepped onto the porch.

"Yes. Pleased to meet you." He respectfully removed his baseball cap and shook her hand. His gaze immediately shifted from her eyes to her stomach, which was bloated out like a beach ball.

Mrs. Oakley laughed. "We're anxious to get moved in, and my husband is working long hours for the Coast Guard. You can see why I can't do too much around here by myself." She patted her pregnant midsection.

The young lady led Billy through the dusty interior. Several rooms were completely vacant. In others, odd albino mountains sat where bed sheets had been draped over furniture.

"Here is the basement," she said, pointing to a five panel wooden door in the kitchen. "I haven't been down there; the steps are too steep for me. My husband says that there is a lot of debris and junk. There are doors that open to the rear of the house, so if you can just get all of the stuff out and pile it next to the garage, my husband will take it from there."

Mrs. Oakley clicked on the light switch at the top of the stairs, and gently closed the door behind the boy. Each of the old wooden steps creaked as he slowly descended. Billy was by no means a timid lad, but he felt quite creepy as he edged his way downward. The cellar had a dank, musty smell that added to his misgivings. He stepped onto the landing at the bottom and peered around the corner. As he panned his view along the cement wall, he gasped audibly at a demon-like shadow on the concrete! He recovered in less than a second though, as he quickly realized that the object that projected the image was only the broken, misshapen remains of a crate.

He laughed off his apprehension, but as he stepped into the room, he jumped again, as a mouse or some other varmint scurried under some old newspapers in the corner.

"I wish I had that slingshot now," he muttered, as he surveyed his surroundings.

There certainly was a lot of junk. There were bundles of old newsprint, boards and planks of various shapes and sizes, old brass and copper pipes, and crates full of old, empty bottles. The walls were bare cement, with two exceptions. At the rear of the house, a half-dozen wooden steps led up to two metal doors. These were obviously the ones that Mrs. Oakley had told him about. At the far end of the room, beyond the sea of debris, was a large but dilapidated bookshelf.

Billy cleared a path to the metal doors and climbed the rickety wooden steps. It took him several hard thrusts with his shoulder to get them to yield. The rusty hinges complained loudly as each of the doors banged open. The sunlight blinded him momentarily, since his eyes had adjusted to the dim cellar. The influx of fresh air and sunshine was a godsend. The basement transformed from a spooky, clammy dungeon into merely a messy room.

The boy spent several hours hauling the rubbish out of the cellar and stacking it alongside the garage as instructed. He was mindful not to lay any debris on top of the square stone cover of the cesspool for fear that in their renovation the Oakley's might need access to it. Finally, he had cleared the entire room with the exception of the decrepit bookcase. He examined the shelves for a moment, scratching his chin. Should he get a hatchet from the garage and smash it into pieces? "First," he thought to himself. "I'd better see if it's mounted to the wall."

He stood to one side for fear that it might crash down on top of him. He grabbed hold with both hands and gave a gentle yank. Much to his surprise, the bookcase neither toppled, nor remained stationary. It actually swung a few inches outward, like a gate. With raised eyebrows, Billy examined where it had moved. There was now a two-inch gap separating the one side from the wall. He slid the fingers of both hands between the case and the wall and tugged again. It moved another inch, but the progress was minimal. Billy braced one foot on the concrete wall and tried again. This time, hidden hinges groaned and the whole edifice spun into the room.

"Well I'll be..." Billy remarked in disbelief. Behind the hinged bookcase stood a large iron door with a sliding metal peep hole about five feet up. There was a mate to this peep hole on the back of the bookcase. It was obvious that both could work in conjunction, and that the basement could be viewed through this sliding window without opening the swinging bookcase.

Behind the hinged bookcase stood a large iron door with a sliding metal peep hole...

The boy examined the metal door more closely. There was a vertical handle where a knob would normally be. Billy grasped it with both hands and pulled. It did not budge. He tried again, tugging as hard as he could, grunting with effort. Yet the door still did not yield. Exhausted, he leaned his back against the cool metal and immediately lost his balance. His arms flailed helplessly as he fell backward into the hidden room.

Billy stood and brushed himself off. "Good one, dumbo," he chastised himself. "Some doors do open *in* after all!"

He peered around him, but could make out very little in the darkness. As his eyes adjusted to the gloom, he was able to see a light fixture hanging from the ceiling. Once he got closer to the fixture he disappointingly noticed that the bulb was missing. The boy scratched his head in thought. Suddenly he snapped his fingers and walked back through the metal doorway, counting his paces as he went. He stopped under the hanging light in the main room of the cellar, and removed his baseball cap. Using the cap to protect against the heat, he unscrewed the bulb. The room fell into relative darkness, but the open metal doors still allowed in enough sunlight to afford a degree of visibility.

Billy retraced his steps to the iron doorway, continuing to count his paces as he slid back into the dark secret room.

"Thirteen, fourteen, fifteen..." he stopped and felt up with his free hand until he located the hanging light. With some difficulty he twisted in the bulb. The gently swinging bulb illuminated the interior.

Billy didn't know what he would find in this secret room, but he was certainly disappointed by the contents.

"Not much to keep secret about," he grunted dejectedly.

The floor was littered with pieces of wood that had once been tables and chairs. Billy estimated that there had once been a half a dozen tables in the room, but they were all shattered and broken. In one corner the remains of an old desk lay in a heap, reduced to splinters like the other furniture. Pieces of what had once been a long counter sat along one side of the room. Mounted on the wall above this debris was a long rectangular mirror, spider-webbed by some violent impact. A large oak beam lay in two pieces on the floor in front of the door. It was obvious that if the beam were still in one piece, it could be placed in slots on the door and wall, in effect locking the portal. Apparently it had broken under some tremendous force.

"I wonder why somebody smashed all this stuff up?" he thought to himself. "Well, it just makes my job easier. I would have had to do it myself to get it out of here."

Gloomy that his discovery had turned out to be so unremarkable, he set about removing the wreckage. He made trip after trip, hauling the material through the secret door and up the rear steps, piling it alongside the garage with the rest of the junk.

As he tossed an armful of wood on the pile, something caught his eye. A white square was outlined on a piece of dark wood. Billy walked over and saw that the square was a folded piece of paper affixed with yellowed tape to what had once been the bottom of a desk drawer. He reached for the fragment and the brittle tape crumbled under his fingers. He began to unfold the paper when he was startled by a sudden rustling noise under the pile. He instinctively jumped back. Regaining his composure, he crept forward. He shoved the paper in his pocket and grabbed a discarded table leg. He poked and prodded the area where he had heard the noise. He nudged a piece of lumber out of the way, and chuckled to himself at what he saw. The unmistakable long hairless tail of a rat hung out from under a flat board. Again he lamented not already owning that slingshot.

But something was not right. The tail hadn't moved. He knew that rats ran for cover if disturbed. Maybe it was dead. But if it was dead, how did he hear it move? The means to answer the question was simple of course. He poked the end of the table leg under the board and tried to flip it over. Because the leg was round it kept slipping, so he leaned over and grabbed the corner and flipped it.

"Whoa!" he shrieked as he jumped back a good three feet.

There, staring directly at him was the triangular head of a big rust-colored snake, the tail of its meal still dangling from its mouth.

Like any typical boy, Billy had been fascinated by snakes a few years before. He read up on them, and even did a report on pit vipers of North America as a school project. A shiver of fear ran down his spine as he whispered: "copperhead!"

The copperhead was rare, but not unknown to New Jersey. It is in fact the most common venomous snake in the eastern United States.

Billy felt that he had to do something. If he ran to get help, the snake would likely disappear before he returned, and he felt that it would certainly be a mistake to allow such a dangerous creature to roam free about the neighborhood.

He swallowed back his fear, and with trembling hands he raised the table leg above his head and crept forward. Slowly he inched within range, fearful that he himself was within striking distance of the serpent. The snake laid motionless, its head and about six inches of its thick body exposed. Billy planted each foot carefully as he moved, wary of slipping on the unsteady debris. He gulped, and held his breath. He knew that if he missed, the reptile would do one of two things: retreat or strike. He gritted his teeth and suddenly unleashed his weapon, swinging down with all of the force he could muster. The blow landed squarely on the snake's head, crushing it instantly.

There was no mistaking that the animal was dead, but from his research Billy knew that recently killed snakes could still strike as a reflexive action, so he was very careful as he removed the remains. He used the table leg and another piece of wood like tongs to drag the body out of the pile. He retreated backward one step, then another, and then another as the snake's corpse continued to slide from its hiding place. Once the entire beast was lying on the ground, he stared in disbelief at its size. It was over four feet long. Still not daring to touch it, he used the sticks to scoot it into a trash can. He then took the can to the curb and dumped the lifeless form down the storm drain.

As he descended back down the cellar steps his feelings were a mix of lingering uneasiness over the danger he had encountered, and pride in his bravery.

"That snake might have bitten some little kid," he commended himself as he continued his work.

At long last he grabbed the last piece of furniture. It was a thin tabletop propped against the far wall. Sweaty and tired, he begrudgingly hoisted the piece onto his shoulder. In his fatigue, he turned quickly, and took two steps before his mind registered what he had seen. He froze in place and slowly turned around. The tabletop had hidden another metal door, similar to the other, but half its size. This one also had the place where a wooden board could lock it.

"I probably carried it out with the rest of the junk," he thought to himself, dropping the old tabletop. He grabbed hold of the handle and pulled. The door creaked open.

A stale odor billowed into his face as he tried to peer past the cobwebs that curtained the entrance. For want of any implement, he used his hand to clear the doorway.

"Yuck!" He tried with great effort to wipe his hand clean on his pants.

Ducking his head, he gazed through the opening. Inside was a brick-lined passage about five feet high. On the wall, inside the tunnel he saw a sconce with a candle in it. He ducked in the few feet to the sconce and removed the candle, quickly retreating from the gloom, back into the secret room.

"I wonder if Mrs. Oakley has any matches," he thought to himself. "Wait a minute!" he snapped his fingers.

The boy skipped through the metal door to the main room of the basement. He held the candle as low as he could and shoved the wick end into the empty light socket. When nothing happened he turned it a bit, trying to ensure that the string touched both the positive and negative terminals. After several moments, his efforts paid off as a flame flickered forth! He quickly withdrew the candle for fear of igniting the fixture.

Billy slipped back through both of the metal doors and into the tunnel. Slowly he crept along the mysterious corridor. There were other sconces along the way, but he did not light any other candles, eager to follow the passage to its conclusion. The flicker of the candle cast eerie shadows on the red bricks, and crackled when the occasional cobweb crossed the flame.

After no more than seventy-five feet, the tunnel ended at a wooden ladder. Billy might have been skittish were he not bubbling with a sense of adventure. He placed the candle in his teeth and began to climb the ancient rungs. His ascent was a short one. The ladder was no more than ten feet high, ending abruptly at a stone ceiling.

Billy ran his free hand over the cool surface. He lifted the candle to inspect it. The stone was whitish in color, square, and not more than three feet across. As he felt his fingers along the edge, he discovered two protrusions on opposite sides, midway across the stone. He brought the candle over for a closer examination.

"There's a rod that runs through it!" he cried aloud.

His arm was beginning to cramp from holding onto the rung, but his excitement eclipsed the pain. On opposite sides of the chimney-like passage, perpendicular to the direction of the rod, two iron pegs jutted from round holes in the brick walls. Each was shaped like an "L." The long end was stuck in the hole in the wall, while the short end pointed upward to rest against the stone ceiling. He grabbed one of the pegs, and it easily slid out. When it did so however, the stone above it swung downward, rotating on the axis of the iron rod running through it. Suddenly the slab sped toward his face, causing him to thrust his free hand up for protection. Fortunately, the stone stopped in an upright position, coming to rest against another protruding iron peg a few inches below the iron bar running through the stone. Due to his sudden recoil, the candle in his hand burned his cheek, causing him to drop it to the ground below where it extinguished.

"Ouch!" He grimaced, rubbing his cheek. But his pain was soon forgotten. Above him he could see wispy clouds floating across the powder blue above. Buoyantly he climbed skyward through the portal.

"Well what do you know?" he said to himself, as he stared at the pile of garbage he had removed from the basement. He

31

glanced back at the trapdoor. "I guess that wasn't the cover for the cesspool after all!"

He carefully piled several boards over the opening to prevent anyone from taking a nasty fall, then climbed the back stairs and rapped on the kitchen door. He was about to knock again when he saw a note with his name on it sticking out of the jam.

"Dear Billy," it read. "I had to run out. If you finish before I get back, please call later this evening for your payment."

The boy rushed to the rear of the house and slammed the metal basement doors shut. He scurried to the driveway and climbed aboard his bike. It was almost dinnertime as he churned his way home. He zipped through the sparse traffic, excited to tell his mother and sister about his discovery.

3

A Secret Message

As Billy zoomed into the driveway he was met with the unmistakable aroma of his mother's meatloaf. The perfume emanating from the oven mingled with the clatter of dishes as he slammed on the coaster brake and skidded to a stop near the open kitchen window.

The boy was through the gate and up the steps in a flash.

Bang! The screen door slammed as he burst into the kitchen.

"Ma! Guess what..." he began.

"William, go out again and come in like a civilized person," His mother scolded, without even turning from the sink.

Billy knew better than to argue. One of his mother's pet peeves was slamming the screen door, and her addressing him as "William" punctuated her displeasure.

"Sorry," he muttered, removing his baseball cap as he slid back outside and reentered "in a more civilized" manner.

"Mom, I gotta tell you what happened!"

"Alright, it will make for nice dinnertime conversation. Go get washed up, and collect your sister. Oh Billy!" She gasped as she turned in his direction. "Take off those clothes right away too! You're covered in dirt and grime!"

Okay Ma." He trudged off to follow his mother's directions, giving the doorjamb a light kick in protest as he passed, still anxious to reveal his discovery.

Ten minutes later the trio was seated around the kitchen table. It was only after the plates were heaped with meatloaf and mashed potatoes and the glasses filled with milk that their mother allowed Billy to recount his adventure. (Although he was sure to omit his encounter with the copperhead since his mother was deathly afraid of snakes. He knew the normally stoic woman would be greatly distressed if she learned of his run-in with the reptile.)

Mary listened without showing much interest as Billy began at the beginning, relating the condition of the room, and where he was to place the trash, etc.

"Big deal," she thought to herself. "Such drama for cleaning out a basement."

Her attitude changed however when her brother revealed the bookcase's secret and the hidden door. Her fork, full of meatloaf, hung suspended inches from her mouth as she stared wide-eyed at her brother. The girl shook off her awe as Billy described discarding the trash from the secret room, and again opened her mouth to deposit the meatloaf when her brother disclosed finding the second secret door. Once again the fork's progress was arrested as she let out a soft "Wow." There the cold piece of dinner remained as the beguiled girl used her mind's eye to follow her brother through the secret passage, up the old ladder, and through the stone trapdoor.

Their mother listened intently and quietly to the whole adventure before commenting.

"That's quite a discovery Billy," she smiled at her son. "Did you tell Mrs. Oakley?"

"I couldn't. She wasn't home when I got through, but I have to go back and get paid, so I'll tell her then. What do you think it means Ma?"

"I really can't say. You know, I'm not originally from this area. I wish your father was home." She pursed her lips. "It seems I once read that the Underground Railroad ran through Cape May. I wonder if that tunnel was used to help hide fugitive slaves."

"Yeah," Billy exclaimed through a mouth full of mashed potatoes. "That's probably it, Ma! We read about the Underground Railroad in school."

"Were there any tracks on the floor of the tunnel?" asked Mary, a quizzical expression on her face.

"What? Like footprints? Gee, I didn't notice any, but it was pretty dark," Billy replied.

"No, train tracks."

Their mother chuckled. "No dear, the Underground Railroad wasn't a real railroad with trains and such. The term 'railroad' was symbolic for the way runaway slaves were helped to escape to freedom in the north."

"Oh," Mary said, slowly chewing a mouthful of mashed potatoes in contemplation of her mother's explanation.

"It must have been scary creeping down that dark tunnel," their mother commented, as she began to clear the dishes from the table.

"I'm going to head back over and get my money. Is that okay Ma?" Billy asked, wiping his mouth with his napkin.

"Yes. Be sure to tell Mrs. Oakley what you found. I don't want anyone falling down that hole." Her words did not hit the mark however, as Billy was already out the door and mounting his bicycle. She sighed and shook her head as the screen door banged shut.

The boy retraced his path to the Oakley's and much to his delight, found the lady of the house at home.

"Oh, Billy come in and sit down for a moment. I have to get my purse," the kind young woman instructed, pointing to a kitchen chair.

"Mrs. Oakley, I have something to tell you…"

"Where did I put that purse?" She put her finger to her lips and scanned the kitchen. "I know. I think it's in the hall closet." She took a step toward the hallway but froze in her tracks when Billy blurted out:

"Mrs. Oakley, you have a secret passage in your basement!"

"What did you say?" The amazed woman returned to face him.

The pregnant lady slid out a chair next to the boy and listened attentively as Billy described his discovery.

"How interesting!" she stated, after the boy had concluded. "I can't wait to tell my husband. He's something of a history buff. A stop on the Underground Railroad, right in our own basement! I'd really like to see that secret room and tunnel myself, but I think I'll wait a few weeks," she said, patting her stomach. "I got word this afternoon that Mr. Oakley will be at sea for another week. So I have a favor to ask. I know you covered the hole by the garage with wood, but I'm afraid that some animal might get down there. If I give you a flashlight, would you mind retracing your steps through that passage and refasten the trap door closed?"

"Sure." He beamed at another chance to explore his find. "That's probably a good idea anyway. I killed a big snake in your yard near the trap door…"

"A snake! Good heavens!" She clapped her hand to her mouth. The panicked expression on her face convinced Billy that he should not mention the type of snake it was.

"Yeah, well I don't think there are any more around," he tried to reassure her. "But if you ever see one, just back away. If Mr. Oakley isn't around, call me and I'll take care of it." His chest swelled as he thought about his battle with the copperhead.

"I will be sure to do that!" she replied seriously, the apprehension slowly leaving her face.

As the mother-to-be fished a flashlight from a drawer, Billy ran outside and dragged away the debris covering the hole so that he would be able to swing the slab into place again. He would have to do this from inside so that he could replace the peg to keep it closed.

He had to click on the flashlight as he descended the basement stairs. The main room of the cellar was extremely dark without either the light bulb or the metal doors open. A pale light bled in through the secret bookcase door as Billy sheepishly realized he had neglected to click off the bulb that afternoon. He stepped through the bookcase door and yanked the pull chain to shut off the light. He again used his baseball cap as a mitt to remove the bulb and dutifully replaced it in the socket in the main room.

Flashlight in hand, he crept back through the hidden room and down the secret passage. He was less excited this time, and was thus able to pay more attention to detail. He scanned the flashlight beam to and fro as he slowly progressed. He determined that the wall sconces held candles at about twenty foot intervals. He examined both the ceiling and floor, which were also made of brick. He was walking with the beam pointed above, scrutinizing the brick pattern on the arched ceiling when he stepped on something that turned under the weight of his foot. A moment later he felt a vicious, cutting pain in his shins. He stumbled forward as his ankles were ensnared and fell violently to the floor, losing the flashlight in the process. Panicking, he thrashed about on the ground trying to free himself from what he guessed was a fiendish booby trap. His momentum caused him to roll several feet down the passage. The flashlight was still spinning on the brick floor as he slammed into the foot of the ladder. A line of pain shot across his back from the fierce impact.

The flashlight came to rest several feet beyond his grasp. It was pointing in the opposite direction, leaving him in blackness. He tried to stand, but stumbled immediately. Lying on his back, he slid his hands down his legs to his ankles and grasped the sinister device. It was a hard metal circle about a foot across. One at a time he slid his feet free and crawled over to recover the flashlight. He had to laugh as he shined the light on the "booby trap." It was nothing more that a hoop from an old barrel. The chance of him getting both feet caught was itself a miracle. He had obviously stepped on the rim, which tilted the hoop upward and as he continued to walk, his other foot threaded itself through the hoop as well.

Billy climbed the ladder, hoop in hand and popped his head through the trapdoor far enough to toss it onto the pile of trash near the garage. He ducked down and pushed on the opposite side of the stone door, swinging it shut. He then replaced the peg and came back through the tunnel, closing all of the doors as he returned. He climbed the cellar stairs and was sure to snap off the light switch before emerging into the kitchen.

"Here you are Billy," Mrs. Oakley said, handing him a five dollar bill.

"Umm Mrs. Oakley, I was only supposed to get three dollars."

"Yes," she said with a twinkle in her eye. "But bravely exploring a secret passage is worth a bonus. Not to mention that snake!" she shuddered at the thought.

When Billy entered the kitchen through the back door, he was careful not to let it slam this time.

"Ma, I'm home!" he cried.

"Oh good." His mother came in from the living room, fastening one of her earrings. "It's my card night with the ladies. Keep an eye on Mary until I return. And also, pick up those filthy clothes you wore to clean that basement. You left them on your bed! Put them right in the washing machine, I don't want them in the hamper with the other clothes. Good bye now," she said, kissing him on the head before slipping out the door.

Billy ducked into the living room to check on Mary. The little girl was lying on her stomach, chin resting on her palms, listening to a radio program. Satisfied that she was alright, he trudged up the stairs to collect his dirty clothes.

Luckily, in his haste to remove his shirt and pants, he had pulled them off inside out, so the filth had not gotten on his bedspread. As he grabbed his pants, he heard a faint rustle. Perplexed, he shoved his hand inside and felt around until his fingers closed around a thick square in one of the pockets.

He removed his hand to see a folded piece of paper.

"Oh that's right," he said to himself. In all of his excitement, he had completely forgotten about the sheaf of paper he had stumbled upon before the snake incident. He unfolded it, but in the failing light of the evening, he could not make out what was on it. He moved over to his desk and snapped on the lamp and flattened the document out beneath the glow of the electric bulb. There were a number of handwritten lines, which appeared to be some sort of a poem. As he read the note his hair began to stand on end.

> *At the rise of the full moon perigee*
> *Stand at Kidd's Treasure Tree*
> *Through the sextant shoot Menkar*
> *Add the degrees on the index bar*
> *Keep your course true and do not stray*
> *Follow to the remains of Sara Mae*
> *50 paces north, as far as you go*
> *To get to the Adventure's cargo*

"A secret message?" he beamed at the thought. "Treasure? Fifty paces? Kidd?" He dared himself to say it aloud. "Could this be directions to buried treasure?"

He bolted down the stairs, message in hand. He raced through the living room, vaulting his prone sister in front of the radio.

"Hey, what are you doing?" Mary asked as her brother scanned the bookshelf on the far side of the room.

"Here it is," He said to himself, ignoring his sister's query.

"Here what is?" she asked. When no answer was forthcoming, she picked herself up off of the floor and danced to Billy's side.

"*A General History of the Robberies and Murders of the most notorious Pyrates* by Captain Charles Johnson." Mary read the deep brown cover of the leather-bound book he had retrieved. "What's that in your hand?" she asked, pointing to the secret message.

Billy was too engrossed to acknowledge his sister. He walked to the dining room table scanning the index as he went. Mary was now curious about what might have entranced her brother, and followed him into the next room.

"Captain William Kidd," Billy stated, triumphantly slamming the open book down on the table.

Mary could see the infamous pirate's name emblazoned across the page. Below the script was a painted rendition of the notorious cutthroat.

As Billy read the biographical article, Mary slid the secret message out from under the book. "Captain Kidd? You think this letter is from Captain Kidd?" she asked excitedly.

"Maybe." Billy brushed her aside as he continued to read.

"Look here," Mary pointed to the page opposite the one her brother was reading. "Do you think this is the *Adventure* the note is talking about?"

"Huh?" Billy roused from his reading and followed his sister's finger to a picture of Kidd's ship *The Adventure Galley*. A chill ran down his spine. "Mary I need a few minutes to read this article. Go and finish your program," he said, pointing to the murmur emanating from the radio in the other room.

"But I want to know what this is all about!" she whined, stamping her foot.

"I'll tell you. I promise. But I need a few minutes peace to read this," he pleaded.

"Okay. If you promise to tell me."

"I do. I do."

Mary skipped back to the radio, and in seconds was again absorbed in her program. Billy closed the door so that he could concentrate on learning what he could about the famous pirate.

As a young man Kidd had been a privateer, a kind of a legalized pirate. The King of England had given him permission to raid the ships of France and Spain in the Caribbean since it was a time of war. After the war, Kidd had moved to New York and married a wealthy widow. He had become a respected member of the community and it appeared that he had settled down to the life of a gentleman. However, he found it hard to shake the need for adventure and when another war erupted between England and France he agreed to become a privateer again. This time he was to attack French ships in the Indian Ocean.

The captain set sail in his new ship the *Adventure Galley* and captured several merchant ships that were sailing under the protection of France. One in particular, the *Quedagh Merchant* was loaded with treasure. Since privateers were able to keep a percentage of the loot they captured, Kidd and his crew had become instantly wealthy. However, there was some question about whether Kidd had legally captured these ships. Kidd thought so, since they had "passes" saying that they sailed under the protection of the French Navy. However, since the ships were owned by merchants from India, some said that Kidd was attacking *any* rich ship he found—essentially that he had become a pirate.

Kidd was forced to abandon the *Adventure Galley* when it began to leak terribly so he sailed home on the *Quedagh Merchant*, which he renamed the *Adventure Prize*. Upon reaching the New World, however, he was shocked to learn that he had been labeled a pirate. He set sail for New York to meet with the governor to straighten out the misunderstanding. Kidd was no dummy, though. What if the governor didn't believe him? In that case he might need to bribe his way out of the mess. So the clever captain buried treasure in several different locations. No one knows where he hid most of his loot, but it is a fact that he was in the Cape May area at the time. The governor of New Jersey even reported that he had chased Kidd's ship in the waters off of Cape May but the "pirate" had out-sailed him and escaped.

Unfortunately for Kidd, the governor of New York sought to make himself a hero by capturing the famous "pirate." He agreed to meet with Kidd to give him a pardon, but when Kidd arrived, he was clapped in irons. Kidd tried to bribe his way out, telling the governor where one of his stashes was buried. However, when the governor didn't release him even after he had the treasure, the captain did not reveal any of his other hiding places. He was shipped to England for trial. Kidd was not allowed to have a lawyer and the French passes he had seized had mysteriously disappeared. Not surprisingly Kidd was convicted and sentenced to death. He made one last attempt to save himself, telling the court that he had over one hundred thousand English pounds of treasure still hidden, and if he were released he would show them where it was.

The court was not swayed, though. Kidd was to be made an example of. He was hanged by the neck until dead, and then his body was locked in an iron cage and put on display as a warning to all "pirates."

By the time the radio show was over, Billy had finished the bio on Captain Kidd. His sister returned to find him sitting in a corner chair, book in one hand, message in the other. He stared at the ceiling, obviously lost in thought.

"Ahem!" she cleared her throat. "Well?"

Billy shook off his meditative state and looked his sister squarely in the eye. "I don't think this note refers to the *Adventure Galley*." This revelation made the girl's features sink into a disappointed expression. "I think it refers to the *Adventure Prize,* a ship Kidd captured. It was full of riches…"

"It's *cargo!*" Mary burst out.

"Maybe…" He tried to put on an air of calm even though he was bubbling over inside. "I may--*may* mind you…have found secret directions to Captain Kidd's buried treasure."

"Pirate treasure!" the girl erupted. "Where did you get it anyway?"

"I found it in the junk from the Oakley's cellar. Mary listen," he became deadly serious. "You can't tell anyone about this. If anyone finds out, we're sunk."

"Not even Mom?" she gasped.

"No, not even her. Besides, it would be a great surprise if you and I could dump a pile of treasure in her lap, wouldn't it?"

"What do you mean? What are you going to do?" The girl's eyes expanded in anticipation.

A look of determination set upon his features. "I plan on figuring out what this means," he said, pointing to the note. "And find that treasure."

4

Captain Kidd's Tree

"Where are you going?" Mary asked from Billy's bedroom doorway.

"The library." The reply was muffled by his shirt as he slid it on over his head.

"The library? What for?"

"I'm going to see if I can find anything about a 'Kidd's Treasure Tree,'" he said, lacing up his sneakers.

"Can I come?" her eyes pleaded more than her words.

Billy thought for a moment. "Okay. But you have to promise not to bother me. Don't ask me a million questions."

A broad grin expanded across the girl's face as she raced to her room to dress.

After a quick breakfast the pair cycled off toward the city library. It was a beautiful sunny day and a refreshing ocean breeze gently nudged them along. They churned their way through the winding streets as the sunlight danced between the overhanging sycamore branches.

A small bell tinkled as the pair swung open the wooden front door. The drapes had all been pulled back and bright sunbeams reflected off of the polished wooden tables, causing the room to actually appear brighter than it had been outside. Billy shaded his eyes to see that they were the only people in the one room library, excluding the very elderly lady behind the counter. Billy bid her good morning as they passed, but she solemnly peered over her half-glasses and put a finger to her lips, despite the fact that there was no one to disturb.

"Nothing at all in this Captain Kidd biography about any 'tree,'" Billy whispered, closing the book in front of him. "Did you find anything in that 'Pirate Encyclopedia'?"

"No," Mary sighed. "Hey, how about those books?" She pointed to the shelf a few feet away. Above the bookcase a small placard read: "Local History."

"Yeah, that's a good idea," Billy praised, mussing her hair. She pretended to be irritated, but in reality she sparkled at any commendation from her big brother.

The boy came back to the table with a half dozen books on Cape May, Cape May County, and Cape May Point. Together they scoured the indexes. Although none mentioned Captain Kidd's Treasure Tree per say, there were numerous entries for the pirate himself. Methodically they paged to each notation and devoured paragraph after paragraph. Most entries were short references to the "legend" that Kidd had buried some of his treasure in or around Cape May, but each was disappointingly vague and nondescript.

"Hey, listen to this!" Billy whispered.

Mary immediately perked up, thinking that her brother had uncovered something about the treasure tree.

"It says here that there's a legend that Captain Kidd buried his treasure in the vicinity of Cape May…"

"So what? We've read that ten times," his sister interrupted.

"Let me finish. The legend says that Kidd came ashore with a half dozen of his crew and had them dig a hole for the treasure chest. After the hole was dug, he made his men draw straws. He then killed the loser and threw the body in on top of the treasure!"

"Why did he do that?" The girl squirmed in her seat.

"So that the pirate's ghost would guard the treasure until Captain Kidd returned for it!"

The girl gulped. She did not share her brother's obvious enthusiasm for such a spooky tale. Anxious to get her mind off of the ghost story, she dived back into the book she had been investigating.

"I found it!" Mary hissed, somewhat above a whisper, bringing an angry stare from the librarian.

"Let me see." Billy slid over next to his sister.

The book was a history of Cape May Point, the town just south of Cape May City. Most of the book discussed the history of the area. The first landowner mentioned was Jonathan Payne, who sold the property to John Stites in 1710. Ship captain Alexander Whilden eventually inherited the land by marrying Stites's sister Jane. Their son, Alexander Jr. became owner with the passing of his parents. But as a young man Alexander Jr. left the shore to open a wool business in Philadelphia. It was in that city that he established a friendship with the wealthy retailer John Wannamaker. At the end of the 19th century, the two decided to build a religious settlement on the site and call it "Seagrove." The town was carefully designed in the shape of a wheel with a great octagonal pavilion at the center, and the streets emanating out from there. Seagrove did not survive as a community, but the City of Cape May Point arose from that earlier village.

None of this interested the readers, but there was a short paragraph that did. It stated that the fresh water in Lake Lilly made the area a popular stopping point for pirates in the 1600s and early 1700s. Beyond this general statement was a reference to Captain Kidd: "...near the lighthouse even stood a macabre and gnarled tree known as *Kidd's Tree*. Old rigging rope draped from its branches where it is said that the vicious pirate hanged one of his victims. The tree was cut down in 1893, but while it stood it was a sinister reminder of a time when pirates prowled the Jersey coast."

"That's it?" Billy grunted irritably. "Swell." He slammed the book closed.

"If that book is right, its not even there anymore," Mary said dejectedly.

They scanned the two remaining volumes without any success. They scooped up all of the books they had used and staggered over to the bookcase to replace them.

"Hsst!" the elderly woman said from across the room.

Confused, they turned in her direction. She snapped her fingers in quick succession and waved them to the counter.

"Yes Ma'am?" Billy asked politely.

"Do not return books directly to the shelves," she whispered.

"They go here." She pointed her bony finger at a small shelf next to the counter adorned with a sign "Reshelving Station."

"Oh, I'm sorry," he said, placing his own stack on the shelf and then helping his sister with hers.

"You know," she leaned close to them and let the faintest hint of a smile cross her lips, "I know where Captain Kidd's Tree was."

"Really?" they questioned in unison. She immediately put her finger to her lips without any indication if it was because they were being too loud, or because she was about to reveal a deep secret.

"Yes," she whispered. "It was cut down more than fifty years ago, but if you climb to the top of the lighthouse you can still see where it stood. After the tree was chopped down, they removed the stump by burning it with hot coals. It actually got so hot that clumps of sand turned into glass."

"Glass?" Mary asked in astonishment.

"Yeah, that's how they make glass. I went on a class trip to Wheaton once and saw them do it," Billy quickly explained, anxious to hear the rest of the story.

51

"Now it's been years since then and the grass grew over the spot. But on a sunny day, if you go to the top of the lighthouse, you can see the sun glinting off of the specks of glass."

"Gee, thanks," Billy gratefully addressed the old woman. She uncharacteristically gave them a wink, then returned to her duties, stamping a pile of cards one after the other in rapid succession.

Mary bounded excitedly onto her bike. It took her a moment to notice that her brother moved slowly, his head down. He wore a grimace on his face.

"What's the matter? We just found a valuable clue!" she chimed in.

"How are we supposed to get to the top of the lighthouse?" he said, venting his frustration by giving his kickstand a hard swipe with his foot.

"Oh," she replied sullenly.

Both were somewhat familiar with the operation and history of the lighthouse since it was a popular topic for grammar school lessons in Cape May Elementary. The current lighthouse was actually the third to be built. It was constructed in 1859 by the Army Corps of Engineers. The man who supervised the construction, George Meade, became famous during the Civil War when, as a general he led the Union to victory at the critical three day battle at Gettysburg. Meade had also designed two other New Jersey lighthouses; one at Absecon and the other at Barnegat.

Originally, the light was fueled with whale oil and later with kerosene. The maintenance and operation of the lighthouse required a keeper and two assistants who lived in small dwellings near the base of the tower. Had this still been the case, perhaps the siblings could have convinced the keeper or one of the assistants to allow them to climb the one hundred and fifty-seven feet to the cupola at the top. However, in 1938 the lamp was electrified, eliminating the need for a keeper. The United States Lighthouse Service was phased out and Cape May's lighthouse, like all others, was transferred to the Coast Guard. During the war, operation was even suspended to prevent Nazi submarines from using it as a navigation tool. The lamp was lighted again in 1945 and the following year a new lens had even been installed. Knowing all of this didn't help them achieve their mission however.

"I have an idea." Billy snapped his fingers. "Mr. Oakley works with the Coast Guard, right? Maybe Mrs. Oakley can get us up there. Let's ride over and ask her!"

"Okay!" Mary concurred enthusiastically. She drove her foot down hard on the pedal, but for some reason she didn't move. The perplexed girl turned to see that her brother had hold of her seat. "What?" she asked.

"Let me do the talking. Remember, I don't want anyone to know what we're up to," he warned.

"Okay, okay," she replied, prying his hand from her seat.

"I mean it, Mary. Don't say a word or I'm not going to let you help me any more. You have a tendency to blabber and this is a top secret project."

"Why hello Billy," Mrs. Oakley greeted as she opened the front door. "And who is this? Is this your sister?" she inquired, bending down as far as her stomach would allow.

"Yeah, this is Mary," he stated curtly, waving his thumb in his sister's direction. "Mrs. Oakley, I was wondering…"

"Hello Mary, it's a pleasure to meet you," Mrs. Oakley cut off the impatient boy.

A panicked look flurried across the girl's face. She gave an awkward nod in response.

"Are you alright dear?" A puzzled Mrs. Oakley pushed further.

"Yeah, she's got laryngitis. Listen, Mrs. Oakley, we were just talking, and it struck us that although we've lived in Cape May our whole lives, we've never been to the top of the lighthouse. I was wondering, since Mr. Oakley is in good with the Coast Guard, do you know anybody that could give us a look?" the determined boy plowed ahead with his query.

"You know what? You're in luck," she smiled. "Last week we had dinner with a Lieutenant Cooke and his wife. He was recently put in charge of overseeing the lighthouse's operation. He is a very nice man, and even spoke about getting a program in place where tours would be given to school children! I'll give him a call this evening. Would that be alright?"

"Gee that's swell Mrs. Oakley! Thanks a million!" He voiced his happiness while his sister expressed hers with a broad smile, still not daring to violate her gag order.

Later that evening the shrill ring of the hallway telephone pierced the home. Billy raced past his advancing mother, his sister close at his heels. He scooped up the receiver and said "Hello" in a single motion.

"It's for me Ma," he informed, covering the mouthpiece with his hand. Their mother shrugged her shoulders and returned to the kitchen.

"Yes. That's right? Really?" Mary could only hear her brother's end of the conversation. "Well, let me see..." He began to excitedly snap his fingers and point down the hall to the kitchen table.

"What?" the confused and annoyed girl responded to his animated gesticulations.

"Hmmm. Let me think..." the boy stalled the caller. "The newspaper!" he whispered, covering the receiver. "Get me the newspaper!" he hissed.

Without further questions, Mary rushed off and was back in a flash.

"Umm, hmm," Billy continued his absurd stalling tactic as he sifted through the pages. "Yes, yes sir tomorrow would be fine. Hmm, well could you make it about noon? Swell. Thank you very much sir."

"What was *that* all about?" Mary asked.

"That was Lieutenant Cooke. Mrs. Oakley came through. He's really into the lighthouse it seems. He's keen about taking us up there. He says we can do it tomorrow."

"What was all that business with the paper?"

"Oh. Well, it's got to be a sunny day right? I was checking the forecast to make sure that tomorrow is supposed to be sunny."

"Wow, that's smart! Let me guess why you made the appointment for noon," said the excited girl, "because that's when the sun is highest in the sky!"

"You know, you're smarter than you look," he chided. "I must be rubbing off on you."

5

Pay Dirt

It was ten-thirty when the duo started off toward the lighthouse. Billy wasn't sure how long it would take them by bicycle, but he estimated forty-five minutes to an hour. He planned on being early, as he didn't want to chance insulting Lieutenant Cooke by making him wait. He was, after all, their only real chance to get to the top of that tower.

They biked down Sunset Boulevard, leaving the city of Cape May behind. Before long the silhouette of the lighthouse was in view. Billy coasted for a second. He shaded his eyes and surveyed above them. The sky was full of blue, but there were also dozens of cotton ball like clouds drifting lazily about.

After about fifteen minutes they made a left off of Sunset and entered the little town of Cape May Point. The lighthouse was still a half a mile away, its stately form looming over the trees. Billy started to get a bit anxious and began to pump the pedals harder the closer he got. The poor little girl tried her best to keep up but eventually had to hail her brother.

"Billy! Wait up!" she bellowed, trailing him by a hundred feet.

Mercifully, Billy slowed his pace. By the time Mary was alongside he braked to a halt. They were almost to the lane that led directly to the lighthouse.

"Why did you stop? I caught up didn't I?" the girl questioned, worried that her brother was angry that he had to slow up.

"I have something to tell you before we meet Lieutenant Cooke, and I can't be sure he didn't beat us here. I'm going to go up with him, and I want you to stay on the ground."

"What?" the girl nearly growled. "No, I want to go up too. You said I could help!"

"That is exactly why I need you to stay down here. The spot is only visible from the top of the lighthouse right? Well if we're both up top, we may see it, but how will we be sure to find it once we get down again? I need you to mark the spot."

"I have a better idea," the little girl countered. "Suppose I go up and *you* stay down and mark the spot!"

"That won't work. First of all, I'm the one who asked Mrs. Oakley and spoke to Lieutenant Cooke on the phone. How ridiculous would it look if suddenly I won't go up? Also, I'm going to have to make some small talk with him without letting him know what I'm really up to. We both know that there's no way that you can do that."

Mary had no choice but to give in. Her brother was of course in charge of this treasure hunt and even more than that, his reasons were good ones.

When Mary made no further protest, Billy began again. "Okay, here's what we're going to do..." he broke off abruptly.

"Good morning," he said, speaking over Mary's head. She turned to see a half a dozen nuns strolling past them.

"Good morning," they replied in the polite, reserved fashion of Catholic Sisters.

"Oh, good morning," the little girl chimed in.

St. Mary's-By-The-Sea was just on the other side of the lighthouse. St. Mary's was a huge beachfront building that had been built in 1889 as the opulent Shoreham Hotel. Despite the hotel's beauty and location, it went bankrupt in 1909. The pastor of St. Mary's Church in Philadelphia purchased the property and reopened the building as a retreat. During World War II the sisters generously leased the building to the Army for one dollar a year. In 1946 the Army vacated, but the sisters were not able to return since the Army's occupation had left the structure in a state of disrepair. A thorough renovation had just been completed and now the sisters once again flocked to St. Mary's to enjoy the sea air. Billy did not speak again until the procession was well out of earshot.

"Here's what we'll do. If I put my left hand out, rotate left, if I put my right hand out, turn yourself right. If I put my hands out in front, move forward, if I put them behind me, back up. If I put both up over my head, that means stop. Got it?"

"Okay. Left hand turn left, right hand turn right, hands in front, means forward, hands behind, I back up. I got it. That's easy."

"What about both hands up over my head?" Billy shot back.

"Oh, did I forget that one? That means stop."

"Good. Don't forget it now."

"I won't."

Billy mounted up and pedaled off down the lane, his sister close behind. It turned out that it was a good thing they had stopped before coming in sight of the base of the lighthouse; otherwise they never would have been able to have straightened out their signals. Even though they were twenty minutes early, a gray sedan was parked in front of the tower. Leaning against the fender was an extremely thin man in a Coast Guard uniform. He waved enthusiastically when he caught sight of them. At first, Billy gauged him to be nearly seven feet tall, but when the boy dismounted and stood alongside him, it became apparent that his height was only about six feet. His extremely slender build created the illusion that he was much taller than he actually was.

"Hello there," he said, shaking the boy's hand vigorously. "I presume you are Billy. And this must be Mary." He removed his hat to reveal his red crew cut and pumped her hand as well.

"I am Lieutenant Cooke as you may have guessed, and this of course is the Cape May Lighthouse." He waved his arm in a grand arc as if presenting a King or Queen.

Billy chuckled under his breath at the odd man's vivacious enthusiasm. "He's sure into this," he thought to himself.

"Shall we begin our ascent? It is after all one hundred fifty-seven feet to the top. You two appear to be in fine shape," he looked them up and down. "That's a good thing, because there are one hundred and ninety-nine steps in the tower's iron spiral staircase," he explained with pride.

"Well, Mary's going to stay down here." Billy's words made the coastguardsman stop short.

"Really? Mrs. Oakley told me two children wanted to go to top of the lighthouse. Are you sure, dear?" His pouty expression betrayed his disappointment.

"She's afraid of heights. She came because she wants to wave to me when I'm at the top." Billy answered for her.

"Very well then," Lieutenant Cooke sulked. "Come on Billy, let's go!" he said buoyantly, as his spirit quickly rebounded. "Just one second, I have to get my binoculars," Billy said, rushing back to his bike and grabbing the case from the wire basket.

"Indeed! Indeed!" the man called after him approvingly.

As Billy ran back to his guide he subtly pointed to the grassy field on the Cape May side of the structure. Mary acknowledged the hint with a nod, and skipped off to await his signals.

As they strode toward the doorway, Billy saw four peculiar large black circles leaning against a shed.

"What are those for?"

"Oh, those," the man laughed. "You're not going to believe this. The other day, I was here doing some work and a couple of boys tied those truck inner tubes together and were planning to paddle it around the point into the Delaware Bay! It's a good thing I showed up to stop them. Do you know how dangerous those rips are?"

The boys in question must have been from out of town, or completely crazy because anyone who lived in the area knew that the "rips"--the place where Delaware Bay meets the Atlantic Ocean-- was no place for amateurs. The sandbars kicked up nasty waves and severe currents. Even a good sized boat could be lost if the captain wasn't experienced.

"These rooms," Lieutenant Cook pointed to two doorways as they entered the base of the tower, "were used to store fuel for the light before it was electrified. The keeper and his assistants had to carry the oil up these steps by hand!" He tapped the iron railing, causing Billy to turn his attention from the storage rooms and cast his gaze up the helix of steps that spun skyward. The boy followed the talkative tour guide up the stairs, half listening as he described the lighthouse's history. About halfway up, a pause in Lieutenant Cooke's speech jarred Billy from his private thoughts.

"Excuse me? What was that?" Billy asked, vaguely feeling that he had been asked a question.

"Do you know how often the beacon flashes?" the thin man queried what he thought was a rhetorical question.

"Umm every fifteen seconds I think," the boy responded.

"Indeed!" the lieutenant was obviously surprised but exceptionally pleased that Billy had answered correctly. "How did you know that?"

"I learned it in school, I think."

"Outstanding! Simply outstanding! You see, I am planning on conducting tours of the lighthouse for local classes. Since teachers are already teaching about the lighthouse, it seems that I should have no problem getting them *on board*, as we say in the Coast Guard!" He snickered at his own joke.

"Lieutenant, did you grow up in a lighthouse or something?" the boy asked, without intending any sarcasm.

Luckily no offense was taken. The man's slender frame shook as he laughed heartily. "No, no. Actually you would be surprised to know that I actually grew up in Nebraska! Can you believe it? I've had a fascination with lighthouses all of my life. As a child, I dreamed of joining the U.S. Lighthouse Service. When it was disbanded I was heartbroken."

They were just about to the top now. In fact, Lieutenant Cooke's foot was just reaching for the top step when he turned to continue his story. "When the Coast Guard took over operation…"

His words hung suspended as tragedy struck. By turning to look at the boy following him up the stairs, Cooke's foot missed the step. He had been gesticulating with his hands, so he had no handhold to save himself. The lieutenant fell forward, his abdomen hitting the edge of the top step. This was not only painful; it knocked the wind out of him as well. The helpless man began to slide down the steps on his stomach, feet first. Almost immediately though, his feet caught one of the stairs, causing him to begin to tumble backward.

Billy had alertly jumped sideways to avoid being mowed down by the avalanche that the lieutenant had become, but just as quickly realized the danger the man was in. He grabbed hold of the iron rail with his right hand and made a desperate stab for Cooke's collar as the man began to tumble backward. His hand caught hold of the coarse material, which fortunately was heavy enough not to tear. The coastguardsman's weight and momentum snapped the boy's arm taunt, causing a pain to knife into his elbow joint. The force was so great that Billy nearly lost his grip on the railing and joined the man in his life-threatening descent.

The lieutenant teetered in a crouched position, the midpoint of both feet precariously balanced on the rim of the step. The boy's uncertain grip was the only thing keeping him from toppling down the remaining one hundred and ninety-five steps. Abject fear was evident in the man's facial expression.

He made a desperate stab for Cooke's collar as the man began to tumble backward.

"Can you... grab... the railing ...please?" Billy spat out between clenched teeth.

As the shock ebbed, reason returned to Lieutenant Cooke. He quickly nodded his head, and took hold of the spiral railing. He then lowered his left foot to the preceding step followed by his right. Once Cooke was stable, Billy released his grasp and the flustered man wasted no time ascending to the landing. He kept right on going and disappeared out the door onto the cupola. Billy followed, and outside he found Lieutenant Cooke sitting cross-legged on the floor.

"Are you okay, sir?"

"I am--thanks to you!" He extended his right hand, which Billy shook. Sweat poured down the poor man's face which had assumed an ashen hue. "Look around son, I...I think I'm going to need a few minutes."

Billy required no further encouragement. He had been concerned about how he was going to explain away signaling to his sister if he in fact could see the spot where Kidd's Tree once stood.

The boy moved around to the side facing Cape May. Nearly one hundred and sixty feet below, five hundred feet to the north he spied his sister waving a vigorous hello. Billy returned her greeting and was just in the process of scanning the field when a shadow draped itself over the lighthouse. He was momentarily perplexed, but swinging his gaze aloft he saw that a huge cumulus cloud had drifted in front of the sun.

"Come on! Come on!" Billy urged, as the gigantic puffy white mass seemed to squat above him.

"Just give me another minute Billy. I'll be okay in a minute," echoed around the curve of the tower.

"T-that's alright sir, I wasn't talking to you. Um, my lens cap got stuck on my binoculars. Take your time, I'm fine."

Finally the cloud decided to move on, and slowly crept on its way. Sunlight gradually swept across the field like a searchlight. Billy's eyes trailed the sunshine as it illuminated the ground below. He scanned back and forth as the rays progressed.

"Aha!" he whispered, as a chill of excitement raced up his spine.

There it was. On the eastern edge of the field a circle of ground began to dazzle. Quickly Billy began to give the hand signals. Right, then forward, forward, keep going! The little girl below moved as if by remote control. He thrust his hands hard several times in the forward indicator. Suddenly he threw both hands up in the air and the pawn so far below came to a halt.

"That's it!" he whispered to himself, pulling the binoculars up to his eyes. He could see the wide grin on his sister's face as she stood atop a small island of sparkles.

6

Navigating By the Stars

Billy lay stretched out on his bed, hands behind his head. He stared up at the ceiling, a sheaf of paper on his chest. Suddenly he grabbed up the page, as he had done at least five times previously.

> At the rise of the full moon perigee
> Stand at Kidd's Treasure Tree
> Through the sextant shoot Menkar
> Add the degrees on the index bar
> Keep your course true and do not stray
> Follow to the remains of Sara Mae
> 50 paces north, as far as you go
> To get to the Adventure's cargo

He stared at the words. "Well now that I know where the Treasure Tree was, what do I do next? Perigee? Sextant? Menkar? What the heck is this guy talking about?"

He threw his hands back behind his head and lay back again. "Wait a minute," he said aloud. "What kind of a dope am I? What am I supposed to do if I find a word I don't know?" He rolled off of his bed and crawled the few feet to the small bookshelf that bordered his desk. He ran his finger past an atlas, an almanac, a set of condensed encyclopedias and a pile of comic books before grabbing hold of the thick dictionary.

"Perigee, perigee..." he muttered, as he thumbed through the pages with one hand and drew up the blinds with the other. "Here we go. *Perigee: The point in the moon's orbit when it is nearest the earth. Antonym- Apogee.* That makes sense. 'The full moon's perigee' is when the full moon is closest to the earth. Apogee is the opposite, when the moon is farthest away."

Eager to know more than the brief definition provided by the dictionary, he ducked down, hauled up the "M" encyclopedia and looked up "Moon." Scanning past the general information on the moon and its topographical features he found some elaboration on the definition he had read: "The perigee and apogee of the moon have a distinct influence on the Earth's weather and tides. When at apogee, the moon is further away and thus exerts less gravitational pull. This often creates more stable weather and tidal conditions. However, during perigee, when the moon is at its closest, the gravitational drag is much greater, often causing tides to be more severe and weather to become less predictable."

Billy scribbled down a few notes on a pad before closing the book. He leaned down to shelve the volume but thought better of it. While he had the "M" encyclopedia out, he decided to look up "Menkar."

"Here we are; Menkar. See Alpha Ceti." Billy exhaled in minor disgust as he had to replace the "M" book anyway. He snatched up the first volume in the row of encyclopedias and found "Alpha Ceti."

"Alpha Ceti is the second brightest star in the constellation Cetus, The Sea Monster. It is also referred to as Menkar from the Arabic for 'the nose' given its placement in the constellation. Menkar is considered a 'navigation star' since it is included amongst the many stars mariners used to plot their courses."

"That makes sense too," Billy was getting excited. "A star that a captain like Kidd would use for navigation, and in a constellation called *The Sea Monster* to boot!"

Enthused that his efforts were bearing fruit, Billy pulled out the "S" book and quickly found an entry for "sextant."

> "A sextant is a navigational tool generally used to measure the angle of elevation of a heavenly body above the horizon. This is called 'sighting' or 'shooting' the object. The angle and time when it was measured can be used to determine one's position on a nautical chart." A picture of a sextant was also shown alongside the description.

"Okay, I've seen one of those before," he said to himself. "I get it now," he became excited again. "*Shoot* in the message means to sight the star Menkar through the telescope part. Then, slide the bar until the star is on the horizon. The gage at the bottom would then align with a particular degree marked on that lower arc!" he said, using his finger to indicate the etched numbers on the picture. "Whatever number it points to, add it to the direction of Menkar, and that shows the direction to head! The time when the measurement is taken is key though..."

He reached for the almanac and opened it atop the "S" encyclopedia, too anxious to take the time to replace it on the shelf. He dug into the book and restlessly scanned through a table showing the phases of the moon for the current year. Along the left hand column ran the dates. In the center was marked the phase of the moon and to the far right the occasional "apogee" or "perigee" notated the satellite's distance from Earth. Since the moon could be in perigee during any phase, Billy searched down to each "perigee" notation and then dragged his finger across to see the corresponding phase. Finally he hit pay dirt. The right hand column listed "perigee" and the center said "full." He continued leftward to the date.

"Good grief!" he burst out. "That's tomorrow night!" His heart leapt in panic. "Okay, okay," he calmed himself, patting his heart. "Getting excited isn't going to help. I need a plan. First, where can I get hold of a sextant?" Billy tapped his finger to his lips. "I know," he snapped his fingers, "Mr. Bradford's!"

Five minutes later, the boy was cycling toward *Maritime Treasures* the little shop owned by Mr. Bradford. Bradford was an acquaintance of Billy's father who had accompanied them on a few fishing trips.

Billy propped his bike against the alley wall and removed his cap as he entered the store. It was dark inside and extremely quiet. There were no other patrons; in fact, he appeared to be completely alone. He had been to the shop a few times before and was always mesmerized by the compellingly creepy atmosphere. Harpoons and spear guns hung from the walls. Shelves were littered with conch shells and driftwood. An old-fashioned diving suit stood in one corner. Wire frames inside held the suit erect, but Billy always imagined that it was the ghost of some lost diver. One glass display case contained items of elaborately carved whalebone, and even some pearls. In the adjacent case were old charts, telescopes, astrolabes and…sextants.

"Is that you Billy?" the voice startled him so much that he jumped.

"Oh, Mr. Bradford. You scared me," he replied to the sandy-haired man who had emerged from the rear of the store.

"I thought that was you. What can I do for you?" the shopkeeper asked.

"I need a sextant," the boy replied, peering through the glass case at several of the instruments.

"Really?" the man laughed. "Planning a trip around the world?"

"How much is that one?" Billy asked, ignoring Mr. Bradford's humor.

"That's a fine one. That's twenty-five dollars." The storeowner had began to slide open the case and retrieve the item when a dejected groan from the boy alerted him that there was no need.

"What's the cheapest one you've got?" the boy nervously pawed at the baseball cap in his hands, fretful that his mission had hit an insurmountable snag.

"This one here," he replied, pulling the tool from the case, "is twelve dollars."

"Oh, okay. Thanks anyway Mr. Bradford." Completely dejected, Billy turned to leave, his head hanging down as if it weighed a hundred pounds.

"Wait a minute," the sympathetic man called after him. "What do you need it for?"

"Oh just an experiment I was planning for tomorrow night," the melancholy boy returned.

"How much money do you have?"

"Five dollars," he replied, pulling out the crisp bill Mrs. Oakley had given him for cleaning the basement.

"I'll tell you what," the shopkeeper said, "you give me the fiver and I'll loan you the sextant. You bring it back in a couple of days..."

"You'll let me rent it? Thanks a million, Mr. Bradford!" The boy's demeanor had done a one-eighty.

"Well, let's not call it renting," the man laughed. "Let's say it's a loan. If you return it in fine shape in a couple of days, I'll give you back your money. But remember, that's worth *twelve dollars* so if you break it or lose it, you're going to owe me the other seven, okay?"

"It's a deal, Mr. Bradford." He shook the man's hand to cement his words. He slid his money onto the counter and turned to leave, but froze in his tracks.

"Something else Billy?"

"Um, yeah. Would you know how to work this thing?"

The man laughed again. "I don't know what kind of experiment you're running, but I can't say I'd wager much on your success. Sure I can show you. Don't you know what I did before I opened this shop?"

"My dad said that you worked over at the Wildwood Naval Air Station." Billy referred to the nearby airbase that trained naval pilots during World War II.

"That's right, but do you know what my job was? It was teaching navigation to new pilots and aircrew," he answered his own question. "You see, what you've got there," he pointed to the instrument in the boy's hand, "is a marine sextant, but sextants can be used to navigate airplanes too. See," he pulled a similar device from the case. "This is an aircraft sextant. It's different from yours in that it uses an artificial horizon to create an angle to measure, where a marine one uses the actual horizon. With yours, you merely find the star you're after with the naked eye. Then you sight it through this telescope part here, then slide it down until the image appears on the horizon. That will give you a reading on the bar here. What is it that you're trying to do exactly?" he asked before going into more detail.

"Well I'm trying to locate a certain star."

"You could do that without a sextant for sure," Bradford laughed.

"Yeah, well the experiment requires a sextant," he replied coyly.

"Okay, I won't pry. What star are you looking for, if you can tell me," he whispered in jest.

"It's a star called Menkar in a constellation called Cetus." Billy tried to reveal as little as possible about his overall objective.

"Sure, the nose of the sea monster."

"You know it?" The boy was more enthused than surprised.

"Of course," he laughed, "I told you I taught navigation. Hold on a minute." Mr. Bradford disappeared into the back room and returned with what appeared to be a dark chart, which he spread out on top of the display case.

"This is a map of constellations for the northern hemisphere. Can you find the Big Dipper?"

"Sure that's easy." Billy easily pointed out the image.

"Good. Now this is Pegasus," he said, indicating a square on the chart. "Do you see its relationship to the Big Dipper? Do you think you can find Pegasus in the sky?"

"Sure, now that I know where it is from the Big Dipper."

"Good. See the bottom two stars in the Pegasus square? Follow those west in a line, and you'll hit the head of The Sea Monster, Cetus." he traced the path with his finger. "The nose, right here," he indicated a particular white dot, "is Menkar."

"Gee, thanks a lot Mr. Bradford. I can definitely find it now!"

"You're a good listener. I wish all of the young airmen I trained were as attentive," he stared off for a moment. "Do you know how many airmen died training over at the Naval Air Station? Thirty-five." He answered before the boy could even open his mouth. "Now some of those were of course due to mechanical failures, but more than one, especially at night, were caused by poor navigation. That's what happened this morning anyway."

"This morning?" Billy asked, puzzled.

"Oh didn't you hear?"

The boy shook his head in bewilderment.

"A fella was flying in from Pittsburg, or Harrisburg... somewhere in Pennsylvania and got himself off course. He eventually corrected, but the darn fool ran out of gas! The guy could've probably landed on the beach, but he was so stubborn that he tried to make it to the airfield on fumes. Well, he didn't make it. He had to bail out and ditch the plane in the Delaware Bay."

"Wow!"

"That's not the end of it. His chute tangled. I'll tell you, the fool is lucky to be alive."

"He didn't die?" the wide-eyed boy interrupted.

"No. He cut it away in time to use his reserve chute. I think he broke a leg. It will be in all the papers tomorrow for sure."

"What do you mean, he *cut it away*?" Billy's curiosity kicked in.

"If there's a problem with the main chute, you can't just pull the rip cord for the reserve see, because it will tangle with the fouled up main chute and you'll go splat." He smacked his palm on the display case to demonstrate his point. "You first have to pull a cord that releases, or *cuts away* the main chute. Once the main chute is out of the way, it's safe to pull the reserve."

The next morning, the incident was indeed covered extensively in the local papers. In fact, it was the buzz of the town as neighbors and friends gossiped about the plane crash. All of this however went right past Billy. He had more important things to think about.

"Billy! Billy!" Mary called, stepping into the back yard.

"In here." A muffled response came from the garage.

"What *are* you doing?" the girl asked, examining the odd contraption her brother was working on.

"I'm rigging it up so that I can pull my wagon behind my bike, see?" He pointed to the forks he had affixed to his rear axel that protruded backward and attached to the handle of his wagon.

"What for?" she asked in a tone that hinted he was crazy.

"You don't expect me to carry a treasure chest home on my handlebars do you?"

"What? You found it?" She grabbed him by the arm.

"Not exactly…" He went on to explain the decoded message and his encounter with Mr. Bradford.

"What about that business about *the remains of Sara Mae?*" she asked; referring to the line of the secret message he had yet to crack.

He shrugged his shoulders without halting work on his bike. "I can't see any way to figure that out, so I'll just head in the direction shown, and keep my eyes peeled. I'm guessing I'll know it when I see it."

"So you're going after it tonight?" she asked, watching as he strapped a duffle bag onto his wagon.

"Yup."

"Can I come?" she asked sheepishly.

"Nope."

"Why not?" the tone of her voice indicated that she was not terribly upset, possibly due to the thought of wandering around at night in search of treasure supposedly guarded by a ghost-pirate.

"I need you to cover for me in case Mom gets suspicious. I'm going to tell her that me and Mike are camping out. *Don't* let her call Mike's house." He gave her a stern look.

Mary replied meekly, "Okay." She watched her brother testing his flashlight in preparation for the adventure that was only hours away.

7

Treasure Hunt

A field of cirrus clouds blanketed the northern sky. Dusk was fast approaching and the wispy swirls painted the horizon shades of pinks and purples.

"I hope that's it for the clouds," Billy said, panning the heavens. The forecast had stated that it would be a clear night, but the boy crossed his fingers nonetheless as he climbed aboard his bicycle.

Mary watched out of the front window as her brother left the driveway. The streetlights were just flickering on as the wagon disappeared down the street.

Billy had hoped to leave earlier, but he had been forced to do a bit of last minute maneuvering to keep his mother from calling over to Mike's house. She was finally distracted from making the call, but by the time Billy had accomplished this, it was beginning to get dark. She insisted that he affix his headlamp to his bicycle before he left. "If she hadn't kept me, I wouldn't have needed the headlight." he grumbled. On further thought however he forgave his mom. "But...I guess I'll need it for the way home anyway."

He continued to make uneasy glances at the sky as he rode, but it seemed that luck was on his side. The stars were slowly beginning to materialize in the clear sky. He had made it as far as Sunset Boulevard, just two miles from the lighthouse. It had become much darker, especially under the trees that lined the road. Suddenly he felt a slight bump and heard a faint hissing.

"Oh, no!" he exclaimed, quickly jumping off of his bicycle. He dropped the kickstand and dove to the ground, pulling his flashlight from his belt. He shined the beam next to him, but it didn't seem to help. The hissing continued. He put his ear to the front wheel and rotated it ever so slowly. When the noise grew louder, he spit on the tire. Sure enough, the saliva began to fizz into small bubbles.

"What am I going to do?" he nearly shouted. He looked around in panic, as if to find a repair kit lying on the side of the road. He froze and snapped his fingers. Digging into his pocket, he yanked out a pack of gum. His fumbling fingers unwrapped the foil and popped a stick into his mouth. "Better use two," he thought, and repeated the procedure. He chewed with determined fury, knowing that time was of the essence. Even if he could patch the hole, he needed to do so while there was still sufficient air in the tire since he didn't have a pump.

"I wish Mary was here," he laughed to himself. "Her jaws flap so fast, she'd have this gum ready in a flash."

He pulled the wad from his mouth and slapped it over the hole. He tried to listen for the leak, but the pounding of his heart seemed to overpower all other sounds. He brought the beam of his light onto the glob of gum and saw that there were still small bubbles seeping out along one side. Quickly he used his thumb to push down on the makeshift patch, spreading it wider. He looked again. No bubbles! He kept vigil over the gum for a full minute before satisfying himself. He pushed on the tire and though it gave a bit, it still had plenty of air. He stepped back to the wagon and rifled through his duffle bag. In a few seconds his fist closed around the ring of electrical tape. He spun the material around the gum a half dozen times.

"I hope that holds it," he mumbled, crossing his fingers as he replaced the roll in his bag.

He saddled up and headed off again, praying that the repair job would hold. By the time he was moving, the strobe of the lighthouse was visible, spinning into view every fifteen seconds.

Billy didn't stop again until he reached the lighthouse. He was anxious to carry out his mission, but he was also afraid to pause to check the tire again fearing an examination might bring bad news. He kept thinking that the handlebars were dipping as the front tire collapsed, but he tried to block it out of his mind. "I'm going to make it!" he declared through clenched teeth, deluding himself that willpower alone could keep the tire inflated.

As he turned into the lane that led to the lighthouse, a giant full moon was rising out of the sea. "Wow!" he let slip. He had never seen the moon look so enormous before. It was so bright that it illuminated the whole beach and ocean. "I don't think ships even need the lighthouse tonight," the boy marveled.

He braked to a stop in the field that bordered the lighthouse. With much apprehension he bent over his handlebars and squeezed the front tire. Much to his relief, the patch was holding fine. He knocked down the kickstand and unhitched his wagon. After the wagon was off, he slapped the kickstand up again and walked his bike over to the high grass and laid it on its side so that it would be hidden from view. He oriented himself with the tower and the lane so that he would be able to find it again.

The night had been very quiet, so much so that Billy was nervous about the sound his kickstand had made. But as he began to drag his wagon toward the general vicinity where Kidd's Tree once stood, a symphony of noise erupted from a nearby marsh. The sudden high-pitched chirping made him jump. "Peepers," he laughed to himself, identifying the vocalization of the tiny frogs.

When he got relatively near the area he and his sister had identified, he crouched low and clicked on his flashlight. He swept the beam back and forth parallel to the ground. Nearly two minutes had passed without success and beads of sweat were beginning to form on the boy's upper lip. Suddenly a bright gleam of yellow flashed a few inches above the turf. He slowly scanned the ray back again. There! There it was again!

Suddenly a bright gleam of yellow flashed a few inches above the turf.

The wagon bounced and rattled behind him as he ran to the spot where he had affixed one of Mary's bike reflectors to a stick and banged it into the ground. It had been a clever method for marking where the infamous tree once grew.

The moon had risen further now. The colossal white orb had crested the old World War II artillery bunker and bathed the field in its glow. It was so bright in fact, that Billy no longer needed his flashlight. He clicked it off and slung it onto his belt. The faintest hint of pink peaked above the tree line to the west, as the sun had all but receded beyond the horizon. Dozens more stars were twinkling on with each passing minute.

He unzipped the duffle bag strapped to the wagon and rummaged through its contents. He removed two items: the sextant and a compass.

He said to himself, "Pegasus, where are you old boy?" as he scanned the heavens. "Ah, there's the Big Dipper..." he stated with satisfaction. "...and there is Pegasus!"

His eyes traced the path from one constellation to the other. "Now for the Sea Monster..." he said, following the bottom two stars in Pegasus westward. "Thar she blows!" he whispered under his breath, identifying the "head" of the leviathan. "And you my friend," he addressed the second brightest star in the constellation, "are Menkar."

He lifted the sextant's scope to his eye. Several times he had to cast his gaze over the instrument and orient himself onto

Cetus again. Finally he "shot" Menkar through the lens. He stuffed the compass into his front pocket so that he could use his left hand to adjust the scope. Slowly he slid the star down to the horizon. With bated breath he removed his eye from the viewfinder and turned the sextant so that he could read the indicator bar at the bottom.

"Ninety-five," he said aloud.

He pulled a small pad from his back pocket and re-read the message he had meticulously copied down.

> At the rise of the full moon perigee
> Stand at Kidd's Treasure Tree
> Through the sextant shoot Menkar
> Add the degrees on the index bar
> Keep your course true and do not stray
> Follow to the remains of Sara Mae
> 50 paces north, as far as you go
> To get to the Adventure's cargo

He fished his compass back out of his pocket and re-sighted Menkar through the sextant. Once he had the star in view, Billy peered down at the dial of his compass.

"One hundred ninety-seven degrees. Okay. One ninety-seven plus ninety-five..." his forefinger stabbed at the air as he calculated, "...two ninety-two. North, northwest!" he exclaimed, examining the luminous markings on his compass.

For a fraction of a second he considered suspending his mission until the daylight hours now that he had the crucial compass heading. However, his excitement was so great that he immediately dismissed the idea as he fantasized about his mother waking to find an overflowing treasure chest in the living room.

"All right Sara Mae, here I come!" the determined boy announced as he stomped off across the field, the rattling wagon in tow.

Billy's progress was far from speedy since he had to be sure to stay on his compass heading. He had no idea how far he might have to travel, and an error of even a few degrees could put him well off course if he had to cover any considerable distance. Therefore, he walked at a steady pace, his eyes bouncing back to his compass every few seconds. In a matter of minutes he had crossed the field and came to a dead stop at the tall reeds that bordered a salt marsh.

Billy sighed, "Oh great."

Not only would it be impossible to carry on with the wagon, but even worse, a marsh could be a dangerous place, especially at night. The water was mostly shallow, but some deep holes hid sporadically throughout and one false step would send him under. The mud could be just as treacherous. In places, the muck could swallow up one's foot or feet and the more they pulled to get free, the greater the suction was created. Billy remembered how the previous autumn a duck hunter had gotten trapped in such a way and wasn't found for three days!

Billy took a seat on the wagon and thought for a minute.

"I probably could go around it…No, if I did; there would be no way to stay on my compass heading. The best I could do is put a marker on this side, and try to line up with it once I was on the other side. No, there's way too much room for error."

He sat drumming his fingers on the side of the wagon for an agonizingly long minute before a solution popped into his head. Snapping his fingers, he vaulted from his seat and dashed across the field toward the silent strobe of the lighthouse.

Suddenly he went flying. Hands outstretched, he took off like Superman, soaring a good five feet before slamming chest first onto the ground. He had the wind knocked completely out of him, but when he could breathe again, he broke out into a fit of laughter. "I guess I did *too good* of a job hiding that bike!" he chastised himself for tripping over his bicycle.

Satisfied that he had hurt nothing more than his pride, he continued on toward the lighthouse, but this time at a more reasonable jog. He slid over to the shed and snatched one of the truck inner tubes. "Hey, this will do nicely too," he grinned, grabbing a rake that leaned nearby. He placed both feet on the rake's head and spun the long wooden handle loose.

He hoisted the handle over one shoulder and rolled the big doughnut across the field, back to the wagon.

He pushed the inner tube down over the wagon. "Perfect!" he exclaimed with delight, as the black circle morphed into an oval and snugged itself under the rim of the cart.

He hauled the duffle bag over his shoulder, pushed the contraption into the water and gingerly stepped into the wagon. "Well I'll be! It works!" he proudly stated, standing upright in wagon's bed. "Now let's see if I can make like one of those gondoliers in Venice." The boy dipped the pole into the water, and struck bottom in less than three feet. He pushed off, moved ahead and then repeated the process. Twice he stopped and checked his compass to make sure that he was still on course, but with no wind and shallow water, he was dead on.

Luckily his path took him across a very narrow expanse of the marsh. It was probably no more than fifty feet, but nonetheless, he breathed a sigh of relief when he reached the other side.

The boy was grateful to leave the wetlands behind. However, what stood in front of him was less than ideal. Before him lie a tangle of brush that bordered a thick forest. "I guess I should look on the bright side," he thought to himself. "The heading could've led me right into somebody's front yard in Cape May Point." He imagined the reaction of a resident who found him digging up their lawn by moonlight and then of him digging birdshot out of his keester.

He unclipped the flashlight from his belt and poked around for a way though the growth. At first, the thicket seemed impenetrable. He swung the light back and forth, then up and down. Luckily, at ground level he found a narrow "tunnel' through the stickers, probably the favorite route of the local rabbits. He had originally planned on leaving the inner tube on the wagon, thinking he would need it for the way back anyway, but there was no way the cart would fit through the passage with the thick rubber ring attached. He labored for several minutes before muscling it off.

Short of breath, but anxious to continue, he tossed the duffle into the wagon and drew it closed to the thicket. He flopped to his stomach and crawled through before emerging in the woods. It had been too narrow to turn around inside, so now he reversed himself and crawled back the way he came. He grabbed the wagon's handle and then crawled backward, dragging the wagon through the "tunnel." He finally made it back through and laid on his back trying to catch his breath. A minute later he popped up, whipped out the compass, and continued the trek.

Cedar trees stood all around him, but as he began to follow the heading deeper into the forest, these were replaced with ancient oaks and towering sycamores. Although the wagon had rattled and jostled behind him in the field, here it rolled silently along. Billy found this so odd; he stopped and bent down to examine the forest floor. The thick foliage above apparently blocked enough sunlight that a thick layer of shade loving moss had carpeted the ground.

The huge moon was almost overhead now, but it was only occasionally visible through the thick canopy of leaves. He was reluctant to use his flashlight, since he did not know exactly where he was, or who or what might be near. He developed a system whereby he clicked it on and scanned twenty feet ahead of him, then shut it off before proceeding. After covering the distance he would repeat the process.

He had left the peepers behind when he exited the marsh, but it was no quieter in the woods. Crickets, cicadas and katydids chimed in for the second movement of the symphony. Billy had often found the song of these bugs comforting as he lay in bed. Their music had the soothing effect of an enchanting lullaby on a warm summer's night. He didn't quite feel that way now, though. Perhaps it was his imagination, but as he moved under the knotted and twisted branches, the sounds seemed spooky; almost like a mocking laughter.

The wind had begun to stir, and the rustling of leaves was added to the noises of the night. The branches creaked menacingly above him. Suddenly, as if by some mystical cue, the insects became quiet. Bewildered, Billy stopped and looked to the canopy above. Although he had found displeasure with the contemptuous clatter, he now wished the bugs would continue. The sudden silence was creepy.

With a resigned shrug, he attempted to shake off the eerie atmosphere and plowed on. The leaves continued to rattle sporadically as the breeze faded in and out. He had gone no more than another quarter mile when he felt an unexpected chill at his back. It was uncanny to feel this clammy, dank wave sweep up behind him. He turned around, curious about the abrupt change in atmosphere. What he saw did little to diminish his uneasiness. A low cloud of mist was slowly advancing in his direction.

It was not uncommon to have fog roll inland from the ocean, but this was different. First, the treetops above him still waved with periodic gusts of wind, and fog usually dissipated under such conditions. Also, this mist was not a high bank, but confined itself to ground level. Certainly fog can form along the ground, but when it does so it normally hangs in patches. This cloud was steadily creeping toward him.

Billy gulped down his apprehension. He checked the alignment on his compass, and continued walking north northwest. He had not gone another twenty feet, however when the white vapor caught up with him. The fog unfolded around him, skulking between the gnarled tree trunks.

His flashlight was now nearly useless, as the beam was swallowed up by the low-lying mist. The sky above was still clear however, and moonbeams continued to filter through the treetops. As the boy advanced, a shape began to form up ahead. Billy approached cautiously. He bobbed his head this way and that, trying to peer around the rings of fog, but only closing the distance seemed to help. After another thirty feet, he could make out huge dark curved spikes, poking through the ceiling of the mist. Closer still he crept.

"What could that be?" he asked himself. "It looks like the ribcage of a dinosaur!" he gasped.

Billy now stood inches from the object. It did indeed look like a giant ribcage, but now that he was on top of it he understood what he had discovered. It was the wooden framing of a longboat. The decrepit remnants were all that was left of an ancient craft, quite possibly an old whaleboat used a couple of hundred years ago.

"I'll have to remember to tell Mr. Bradford about this," he noted, seating himself on one of the antique timbers. It felt good to rest for a moment, but he was still no closer to finding the remains of Sara Mae. He hauled himself up again and was about to continue his north-northwesterly trek, when something else caught his eye. A dozen feet to his left, a series of irregular objects jutted up out of the fog.

Full of curiosity, the boy prowled up on one of the objects and ran his hand over the rough bleached surface. Kneeling down, he brought his face within inches of the thing and illuminated it with his flashlight.

"John Trumbell, b. 1722- d. 1778," he read. "A graveyard! An old lost graveyard!" he called out. "This could be one of the old whaling communities! Mr. Bradford is sure going to be glad he loaned me that sextant, this is like an archeological find!" He was pleased that he had pronounced the word "archeological" correctly.

The boy picked his way through the fog to examine the two dozen headstones, pausing only long enough to read the name of the deceased. Suddenly he froze. "Sara Mae Jorgensen," he whispered, running his fingers over the engraved name. "If you weren't a skeleton, I'd give you a kiss," he joked, pulling the pad from his back pocket.

He read the secret message again. "Fifty paces north." Billy put the pad away and danced back to the wagon to retrieve the duffle bag. He crouched down, unzipped the bag and pulled out the folding metal shovel his dad had gotten at the army-navy store. The boy consulted his compass and faced north. "Kidd was about six feet tall, so I'm going to have to take extra big strides to match his." He took a deep breath and counted off his exaggerated steps until he reached fifty.

His paces terminated in a very small clearing, no more than five feet by five feet. This small area was bordered on two sides by large boulder-like rocks and on the other sides by two ancient trees. One was a sycamore, it's peeling trunk four feet in diameter and the other was a black walnut, every bit as big as the sycamore.

"Well, I couldn't be off much. This is the only spot possible to dig,' he said aloud.

He drove the spade into the ground, and threw the dirt past the trunk of the sycamore tree. As he did so, his field of vision extended around the trunk. He was replacing the head of the shovel in the ground when his brain caught up with his eyes. Did he see something moving beyond the trunk?

Foregoing another shovelful of earth, he poked his head around the ancient tree. His hair stood on end. Some forty feet away, it was visible through the swirling vapors of mist. A translucent, ashen apparition thrashed angrily toward him!

Immediately the story of the ghost-pirate who guarded Kidd's treasure rushed into his head as he fell backward against the huge rock, trembling in fear.

8

Digging up the Past

Billy lay with his back to the boulder, his frightened fingers trying to dig themselves into the rock. At any moment he expected the phantom to emerge from around the tree trunk and seal his fate.

Yet, nothing happened. Ten seconds had elapsed, then twenty... Slowly he removed himself from the stone face. Silently he bent down and retrieved his shovel. Billy adjusted his grip on the handle and drew his hands up over his head, ready to chop down with all his might should the spirit materialize in front of him. With measured steps he crept forward. He paused with his back to the sycamore and drew in a deep breath.

With a leap he cleared the side of the tree but the ghost had still not approached. Through the fog he could see the apparition still flailing in the distance. In fact, it looked as if it was straining at some invisible bonds; as if some unseen force had kept it from advancing upon him.

Surviving impending doom had emboldened the boy. He stalked toward the ghostly form, his shovel still poised for action. Beads of sweat began to race down from his brow as he slowly advanced. The specter's appendages seemed to reach out toward him as he slid onward through the swirls of mist. He was nearly on top of the spirit when he began to laugh.

"A parachute!" he burst out. "It's just a parachute!" The thin cords from the chute had become entangled in the brush, allowing it enough slack to move in his direction when the breeze caught the material. The wind likewise caused the folds of silk to oscillate, accounting for its ghostly dance. "I bet this belongs to that fellow who crashed his plane into the bay," he thought to himself, recalling the story Mr. Bradford had told him.

After debunking "the ghost" he was upbeat once again. He turned and jogged back to the hole he had begun. As he trotted, the mist seemed to evaporate in front of him. The insects began to chirp again, and a warmth spread over the woods, completely dissipating the fog. It was as if the whole atmosphere of the forest imbibed in his relief.

Forty-five minutes later Billy was up to his chest in a pit. "How deep could it be?" he grunted angrily, as he knifed the shovel back into the ground. After another twenty minutes the exhausted boy leaned against the side of the hole. "Something's not right," he sighed. "Fifty paces. *I made fifty paces.*" He shook away his doubts. "These trees have been here forever," he said of the two huge trees bordering his dig. "And these rocks certainly aren't new. There's simply nowhere else to dig!" He banged one of the boulders with his shovel. "Hold up," he said to himself as an icy thought raced through his mind. "What if there's *another* Sara Mae buried over there."

Billy scurried out of the hole, back to the forgotten cemetery. He couldn't be sure which markers he had already examined so he scrutinized each, one at a time. Methodically he moved from one leaning headstone to the next. Although some were crumbling, and others faded, luckily all of the wording remained visible.

"Nope, no other Sara Maes," he stated after his last inspection. He sauntered back to the hole, and sat atop the pile of earth he had excavated. "I just don't get it!" To punctuate his frustration, he heaved a golf ball sized rock into the forest.

"Dong!" A metallic note rang out through the woods.

"What?" bellowed the startled boy.

He leapt over the pit and walked in the direction he had thrown the stone. He swept his flashlight in front of him as he moved, and was surprised to find that he was back at the ruins of the old boat. "What's that?" he ejected, as his passing beam glinted off of some object. Billy brought the light back toward the reflection and gingerly stepped through the wreckage. He picked through the timbers and hauled up the relic. It was an old bell, about twice the size of his hand.

"Maybe I'd better take this back," he thought. "Mr. Bradford could probably sell this in his shop."

He studied the piece with his light, turning it to see the other side. His heart fell to his knees when he read what was inscribed on the surface: *Sara Mae.*

"The boat! The boat!" he stammered out. "*The boat* is the Sara Mae!" he fumbled for the pad in his pocket. He read the lines again, "'Keep your course true and do not stray, follow to the remains of Sara Mae.' The remains of the boat!"

He danced back to the duffle bag and tossed the bell inside. The compass was out of his pocket before he had even made it back to the skeletal longboat.

"Okay. North it is," he mumbled, orienting himself with the needle. He was about to take his first step when a distressing thought swooped into his head. "How do I know where to begin? Do I start at the bow or the stern? This boat is long enough that it would make a big difference!" He pulled the notepad out again and reread the lines, though he already knew they did not discern any more than "the remains of Sara Mae." He leaned against an intact remnant of the gunwale and thought for a moment.

"Well," he finally concluded, "I'll try pacing it out from the stern, bow, and mid ship and see where each leads. I hope I won't have to dig a hundred holes."

He began in the stern and followed the heading for forty-eight exaggerated steps. He was unable to complete the remaining two however since a large boulder, like those near his first dig site, impeded his progress. "Well that's a lucky break, it eliminates that spot."

He next stood halfway up the length of the rotting keel and repeated the process. At fifty, he swung his flashlight beam to his feet. "I guess this could be a possibility..." He grabbed a nearby stick and marked the spot by jamming it into the earth. "Now for the bow..." his words were cut off. He had turned to walk back to the boat and after only one step, stubbed his toe and fell face first to the ground.

"Stupid roots," he muttered as he shone his light on the culprit. However, it had not been a root that had upended him. It was a flat, hard plank from the Sara Mae. He had obviously cleared it on his way out from the boat due to the giant "paces" he was making. He kicked at it in retribution. "Ow!" he exclaimed, rubbing his foot. He picked up the board to find that it had practically petrified. The end of it was discolored, stained a chocolate brown. Instinctively he shined his light on the ground. The earth was jagged and furrowed. The ground was hard, but bumpy and it formed a shallow mound, slightly higher than the ground around it.

"I think somebody dug this up!" he concluded with a hopeful burst. He examined the ground with more care and slid his fingers into a depression. It was about six inches wide and one half inch across. A flash of recognition washed over his face. He looked at the plank he held, and gingerly inserted its end into the rut. "Somebody used this board to dig!"

He laid the wood flat to mark the spot and hustled back to retrieve the shovel. Less than a minute later he was eagerly chopping away at the compacted mound. Vigorously he scooped out the earth. Before he knew it the mound had disappeared and he was cutting into the dirt below. He was two feet deep when his spade struck something solid.

The boy was nearly shaking with energy, bursting to tear away at the earth, but he knew he had to proceed with caution to avoid destroying whatever lay beneath. With great difficulty he bottled his verve and flipped over the shovel so that the blade pointed downward. He ducked down and outlined the object with his forefinger. It was approximately eighteen inches long by twelve inches wide. He bathed it in the beam of his flashlight, and used the palm of his hand to brush away the earth. He formed his hand into a fist and rapped on its surface. "It's made of wood," he concluded.

With effort he continued to restrain his recklessness and methodically dug away at the soil surrounding the object. He had uncovered five inches of its depth thus far, and by now it was clear that it was an old wooden box. He laid his shovel aside and traced the outline again with his hands, brushing away any loose dirt. As his hands slid along the short sides, his fingers fell into oval holes, one on each end.

"Handles?" he guessed in surprise.

Less than a minute later he was eagerly chopping away at the compacted mound.

He slipped four fingers from each hand into the slots and crouched, straddling the box. Slowly he contracted his arms in an attempt to remove the chest. However, it did not budge. The many years spent in the ground had cemented the bottom to the earth. He rested for a moment and then gave it another try. He was more practical this time, lifting more with his legs than his arms. With a start, the soil holding the crate gave way and the box jolted upward.

Billy fell backward, tripping over the edge of the hole, the contents of the mysterious chest tinkling as the box came to rest in his lap.

For a long moment the boy sat in the pale moonlight, staring at the container. Shock, awe, satisfaction all swept over him. He'd done it. He had actually done it! People had been whispering about Captain Kidd's buried treasure for two hundred and fifty years, and he had found it!

Billy gently placed the box on level ground and retrieved his flashlight. He felt around the top of the chest and discovered a small lip hanging over the perimeter. He rested the flashlight on the ground, pointing the beam toward his discovery. He gently dug his fingers under the lip. With a careful yank, the cover came free.

He stared at the contents, unable to believe what he saw. He stood openmouthed for a full ten seconds and rubbed his eyes. Could it be? Was this really what he was seeing? He dove for the flashlight to confirm his suspicion. The light revealed twelve small circles protruding upward. He reached down below one of the rings and wrapped his hand around the smooth neck and lifted the object out of the crate.

"Booze?" He blinked in disbelief. "A crummy case of booze? You have got to be kidding!" he sputtered in disgust.

Billy sank down on the ground holding the tall bottle, staring blankly at the flask. Suddenly hope bubbled up again. "Wait a minute! I haven't checked the bow!" He replaced the bottle in the case and tore off toward the front of the ship. He turned until the compass read zero degrees and marched off to the north. Unfortunately, this measurement terminated inside the trunk of a big oak, eliminating the chance that there was any treasure beyond the case of liquor.

"Well, at least Mom and Dad will be able to have wine with their dinner for a while," he thought, as he tossed his tools back into the duffle bag.

It would be hard to say whether the boy was more exhausted or dejected as he dragged the wagon back through the forest. Laboriously he crawled backward through the thicket, dragging the case of wine behind him. He crouched down again and repeated the process with his wagon. He tried in vain to suppress a yawn. He contemptuously shook his head to clear the cobwebs, knowing that there would be time for rest once he got home. He snatched up the inner tube and reassembled his amphibious wagon. Carefully straddling the case of wine, he poled his way back across the bog.

A faint pink was edging over the eastern sky as he slogged out of the marsh. Too tired to struggle with removing the inner tube, he pulled out his pocket knife and slashed at its wall. The ring quickly collapsed into a pile of rubber. The bottles clanked noisily as he dragged the wagon toward his concealed bicycle.

The sun had now cleared the horizon and was dazzling off of the rolling Atlantic. Billy let loose another loud yawn as he climbed aboard his bike. As the worn out boy pumped the pedals homeward, he was so weary he didn't even think to worry about the bubble gum patch keeping the air in his front tire.

The sleepy boy mechanically cranked his way home. The streets were bare except for those whose jobs brought them out in the early hours of the morning. In the center of town he passed the milkman loading his truck. As he groggily rode by the newspaper office the big overhead door clattered upward, shaking him back to consciousness. A burly man tossed bundled papers to the curb ready for pick up. As he turned down his own street exhaustion had crept up on him again and he barely noticed the sedan that passed him, and was completely oblivious of the man in the passenger seat who turned to view him through the rear window.

He quietly coasted up the driveway. Too beat to unhook the wagon, he swung off of his bike and walked the makeshift vehicle into the garage. He left the crate and duffle bag, and trudged around the side of the house toward the lattice leading up to his bedroom window. He was two rungs up when a gentle

"Ahem!" stopped him cold. He looked through the trellis to the adjoining front porch to see his father leaning against the house, arms crossed.

"Billy, I think you'd better come over here," he said in an authoritative voice.

The boy was too tired to even formulate an excuse. He lumbered around the porch and climbed the steps.

His father's hands were dirty and he wore stained overalls. "I guess you didn't notice Mr. Brown's car pass you up the street, he just dropped me off. Have a seat." He pointed to the porch swing. "I believe you have some explaining to do."

Billy trusted that his father would understand his actions once he knew the truth. He began at the beginning and before he had even progressed beyond the secret message, his father pulled a rocking chair up to listen more intently. Telling the tale seemed to rejuvenate him, especially when he saw that his father was far from angry, and actually rather engrossed in the adventure. The man did not interrupt, not even once, even though it took the boy forty-five minutes to recite the whole story.

As Billy finished, the clatter from the kitchen drifted through the open front windows proving that his mother and sister were now awake.

"Where is that case now? In the garage?" his father asked.

"Yeah Pop, its on the wagon."

"Go inside and get a shower. And get some breakfast, you must be starving," his father said hurriedly, and abruptly stormed into the house.

Billy was bewildered by his father's haste, a confusion that was soon shared by the rest of the family. He could hear their voices spill through the house.

"Oh, hello dear, did you just get back..." he heard his mother say.

"Um yeah, where are the car keys?" his dad cut her off.

"In my purse. Why? What's wrong?"

"Nothing's wrong, I just have to run out for a bit. I'll be back soon."

Billy heard the keys jangle and the back door bang. As he wandered into the house, he could see the driveway through the side window. The trunk of the car opened, and then closed. The engine roared to life and a moment later the sedan spun out of the driveway.

Billy snuck upstairs and showered before his mother discovered that he had been out all night. As he toweled off, the enticing aroma of bacon and eggs wafted up the stairs. He tied the towel around his waist and went to his bedroom. The urges of fatigue and hunger played tug-o-war with him. Finally he tried to reach a compromise, "I'll just lie down for a minute, then I'll eat..." As soon as his head hit the pillow he was out like a light. Fatigue had won.

"Bang!" the slam of the kitchen door shocked him back to consciousness. For a moment he didn't know where he was or even who he was for that matter, such was the depth of his slumber.

"Bill, where did you go? And how many times have I asked you, please don't slam that door," the boy heard his mother scold his father.

"Forget about that, where's Billy?" his dad broke in hastily.

"Still sleeping I guess…"

"No, I'm right here." He emerged at the bottom of the staircase after having thrown on a pair of shorts.

Mary poked her head from the kitchen, her eyes pleaded at her brother. She was bursting to know what had happened the night before. However it wasn't her brother who dropped the bombshell, it was her father.

A broad grin spread across his face. "We're rich," he said.

9

A Different Kind of Treasure

"Rich? What are you talking about?" Their mother chuckled, assuming their father was joking.

"You found it? You really found it?" Mary bellowed, shaking her brother by the arm.

"No, I didn't." The confused expression he wore said as much as his words.

"You didn't find Captain Kidd's treasure?" Mary asked, astonished after her father's declaration.

"Captain Kidd's treasure? What *are* you talking about, Mary?" their mother questioned.

"I haven't had a shower yet, and I'm sure that you wouldn't appreciate me sitting on your nice couch with my fishing clothes, so you three go into the living room. While I get cleaned up, Billy you tell your mother the story you told me," their father directed.

"But, what about being rich?" Billy begged for explanation, but his father had already disappeared up the staircase.

Billy gave their mother a hurried, abbreviated version of his story and kept glancing up the staircase as he spoke, anxious to hear what his father had to say. Mary tried to interrupt him many times; both with accounts of her own participation in the adventure and also with questions regarding the night that had just passed, but the boy merely spoke over her, unwilling to prolong the tale. His mother cast several disapproving expressions his way, particularly when he described lying about camping to hunt for the treasure, but she did not interrupt him. He had just finished when a cleanly shaven and neatly dressed chap shuffled down the stairs. Their father looked like a new man.

"Okay, is everybody up to date?" he asked the six anxious eyes that peered at him.

"Yes!" both children nearly shouted.

He chuckled at their impatience, but it was obvious that there was more to his merriment than his kids' enthusiasm. He settled himself into a chair before beginning.

"When I was a boy, the house where you found that tunnel was owned by Robert Bennett. Now when I was around your age, Billy, in about 1930, it was the time of prohibition."

"What's prohibition?" Mary asked.

"In 1920, the Eighteenth Amendment to the Constitution was passed making it illegal to buy, sell, or transport, liquor," her father explained.

"It's not like that now though," the little girl stated.

"No, in 1933, it was repealed by the Twenty-First Amendment."

"Why?" Mary asked.

"Well, basically because it didn't work. People drank anyway, and even though the government tried hard to stop them, it just wasn't possible."

"If it was illegal, where did they get it?" she questioned further.

"Well from different places. Some made it themselves in devices called 'stills.' There were more than a few stills hidden in the woods around here. Since the stills had to be run at night to avoid being found, their operators were called 'moonshiners.' But living where we do, the easiest way was from rum-running. You see," he anticipated her next question, "three miles from shore was the limit of U.S. jurisdiction, so large ships from Canada, or the Caribbean, or Europe would anchor just beyond the three mile limit and rum-runners would take their boats out, buy booze and bring it back to sell themselves. So many people were rum-running that the government pushed the line back from three to twelve miles in 1924. This caused some to give up, but others were more determined. Robert Bennett, who used to own the Oakley place, was one of those persistent rum-runners."

He continued, "That secret room you discovered," he said to Billy, "was a 'speakeasy.' A speakeasy," he now turned to Mary, "was a secret saloon. Since the real ones all had to shut down, a lot of saloons and nightclubs were relocated to hidden rooms.

111

That tunnel Billy discovered was an escape route in case the police raided the place."

"What about the secret message?" Billy asked.

"You really thought that was about Captain Kidd's treasure?" He chuckled, and the boy's face flushed with embarrassment. "I shouldn't laugh," he consoled. "That was some pretty nifty figuring you did, and you solved a mystery as legendary as Kidd's--at least in these parts."

"You see, Bennett began as a moonshiner and rum-runner. As his business grew he opened a speakeasy. But he progressed into more than that. He had made connections that would supply him with expensive and rare wines that he would then sell to wealthy customers in Philadelphia."

"How do you know all this?" Billy asked.

"Gee Billy, if you grew up in this town at the time, you knew. *That* was no mystery. The mystery began one night in 1930. Bennett had gone out in his boat *The Adventure* to pick up an especially important shipment..."

"The *Adventure*?" Billy interrupted. "And here I thought the note referred to Kidd's ship the *Adventure Prize*!" he scoffed at himself.

His father continued, "I guess that was logical since you had Kidd on the brain from that 'Treasure Tree' bit, but *Adventure* is a very common name for boats. There are probably four in Cape May harbor right now. Anyway, he made the pick up, but this time the Coast Guard had laid a trap for Bennett. They tracked him back in past the twelve mile boundary and gave chase. Most people assumed that he had thrown over his cargo, but now we know he didn't. He must have thought it way too valuable, which probably explains what he did next. He aimed his nose at the lighthouse and ran straight for the beach. He knew that the Coast Guard would never purposely run their cutter aground. At worst, they would come in as close as they dared and send a skiff after him. But that would take time, and he hoped to be long gone by then. He beached his boat near where the artillery bunker sits now, grabbed the case and hid it."

"After he had hidden it, he ran home as fast as he could. What he didn't know, was that the Coast Guard was part of a bigger operation against him. By the time he was in the secret room in his basement, Prohibition Agents from the federal government were pulling up outside. He escaped, probably through that tunnel you found, but was caught a few blocks away. The Feds put him in the local jail for the night and in the same cell was Milt Hendricks, a friend of your grandfather's."

"Why was *he* there?" Mary asked.

"Oh, I don't recall. Milt was a good old boy, but he never shied away from a fight. He probably got into a tussle down at the docks or something. Anyway, Milt said that Bennett was cool as a cucumber. Bennett told him that he had left directions for his lawyer where he would find 'something worth enough to not only get him out of jail, but allow him to retire as well.'"

"That story circulated for years..." he trailed off in remembrance. "But, Bennett died of a heart attack before he even met with his lawyer."

"Wait a minute," Billy interjected. "Why did he leave such a complicated message? Wouldn't it have been easier just to tell his lawyer when he saw him?"

"That Bennett was a strange bird. He was the secretive type and I suppose that he was afraid that the cops or Prohibition Agents might listen in," his father answered. "Remember how important that crate was to him--he was planning on making enough from it to retire. Plus," he shook his head and laughed as if recalling some long forgotten stories, "he was a real eccentric. He loved puzzles and such."

"Those were pretty complex directions to come up with spur of the moment like that though," Billy puzzled.

"Not as much as you might think. Bennett had served as a captain in the Merchant Marine. He was completely familiar with navigating by the stars. Shooting that star with the sextant would have taken him all of two seconds. He knew those woods like the back of his hand too. After all, in the early days he had stills hidden back there."

"So, when I told you my story, you knew what I had found," Billy stated.

"I was pretty sure. I ran over to see Mr. Wilkes." Wilkes was a restaurateur in town whose establishment catered to wealthy tourists in Cape May. He had originally operated an upscale restaurant in an affluent suburb of Philadelphia, but always summered in Cape May and for about ten years now had been running another high class eatery in town. Billy's father sold fresh fish to Wilkes, so they were already acquainted. "Mr. Wilkes nearly fell over when I showed him the bottles. Did you read what was stamped on them?" he asked his son.

"No, I didn't." he confessed.

"Well, it wouldn't have meant anything to you anyway," he laughed. "It certainly didn't mean anything to me until Mr. Wilkes explained it. What you found is a kind of wine called *Madeira*. It's made on a Portuguese island. Not only is it rare, but it seems that most wines spoil after twenty or thirty years, but Madeira is just reaching its prime when it hits the century mark. Did you see the year--oh that's right," his father caught himself; "you didn't read the stamps. This Madeira was bottled in 1852, nearly a hundred years ago. *And*, it appears that it was stored in precisely the correct way. Since it was buried below the frost-line, it was kept steadily at the perfect temperature."

"What is it worth?" their mother quietly asked.

"Well, Mr. Wilkes wanted to buy the case outright for $35,000..."

"Thirty-five thousand dollars?!" the three listeners exploded in unison.

"But," his father continued, "He confessed that at auction the wine could fetch as much as eight to twelve thousand per bottle."

"What?" their mother gasped, covering her mouth with her hand.

"He offered to act as our agent for a modest percentage. Later I'm heading over with Hanson, you know, the lawyer, to draw up a formal contract."

———————————

"So, it wasn't pirate treasure after all?" Brooke asked.

Mr. Jacobs chuckled, his neat white beard hiding his smirk. "Well, I guess not pirate treasure exactly...more like smuggler's treasure."

"How much did they get?" Max asked their host.

"All told, they pulled in something like $110,000."

"Wow!" Brooke gasped.

"And you have to remember," Mr. Jacobs furthered, "that that amount is akin to almost $900,000 today."

"Boy, that's an awful lot for twelve bottles of wine." Max shook his head in near disbelief.

"Well, it wasn't actually twelve bottles. The family kept one as a memento..." Mr. Jacobs was interrupted by a knock at the door.

Brooke spun on the couch and peered out the window. "Mom's back!" she called out, following Mr. Jacobs to the entranceway.

"Mommy!" his sister yelled as the door creaked open.

"Hi there, were you good for Mr. Jacobs?" he heard his mother ask.

Max got up to greet his mother, but stopped abruptly. He froze in place and a chill swept over his body. "Could it be?" he asked himself. The conversation from the hallway disappeared as his attention fixated on the object. As if stalking prey, he crept across the room to the shelf and ran his fingers over the old bell. "Sara Mae," he whispered, reading the inscription. He jumped over to the brown bottle resting nearby. The embossed lettering leapt out at him—*Madeira 1852*. He slid his eyes over to the framed degree hanging on the wall. "Upon the recommendation of the faculty, the Board of Trustees hereby confers upon William R. Jacobs the degree of Bachelor of Arts..." As if in a trance, he walked across the room to the picture of the little boy and girl. He slid the bouquet of dried flowers away from the base of the frame. "Billy and Mary" was written across the bottom of the photo in faded ink.

"So, did you make out okay?" Max's mother jolted him with her question. "The rain's stopped, would you like to go up to the arcade?"

"You..." Max gazed at Mr. Jacobs, amazement written across his face.

The old man was standing behind Brooke and his mother, so they were unaware when he gave the boy a smile and a wink, before bringing his forefinger up to his lips.

Max smirked knowingly and returned a subtle wink. "Um, what was that?" he turned to his mother.

"Do you want to go to the arcade?" she repeated.

"No, I was thinking that "adventure weekend" idea wasn't such a bad one. I have some ideas about where to explore too. There is an old abandoned graveyard, and if the sun comes out, we should go to the top of the lighthouse..."

"Oh yeah, that would be cool, we should do that!" Brooke broke in, shaking her brother's arm.

"Well okay," their mother chuckled at their zeal.

"Mom, did you know that Captain Kidd might have buried treasure right here in Cape May?" Max asked, as the trio crossed the threshold.

"Is that right? Well that might provide an opportunity for an adventure in itself, huh?"

"Oh yes," Brooke bounced excitedly in front of her mother. "It's still out there waiting to be found!"

Max and his sister began to impatiently sputter out Kidd's story as they continued onto the porch.

As the children dragged their mother down the front walk, she was able steal a glance back over her shoulder in time to exchange a knowing smile with Mr. Jacobs before he closed the door.

The End

More books by Steve Leadley:

Sherlock Holmes in Cape May

A Victorian Romance in Cape May

A Doo Wop Mystery: A Nostalgic Wildwood Story

Check out these and his other books at:

steveleadleyauthorpage.weebly.com/

or look for him on Amazon.com